KARMA'S SPELL

MAGICAL MIDLIFE IN MYSTIC HOLLOW: BOOK 1

LACEY CARTER   HELEN SCOTT   L.A. BORUFF

DEDICATION

To our amazing readers who just want a handsome bear shifter in their lives, and maybe even a pack of best friends to make you laugh.

1

EMMA

My phone started ringing and I groaned, reaching for where it should've been on the nightstand. Instead, I lost my balance, rolled off the bed, and hit the floor, knocking the air from my lungs. When I could manage to make a sound, it came out something like a sad cow, and my eyes flew open.

Okay. I wasn't in my bedroom. I was lying on my normally neat living room floor, but underneath me was the unmistakable crunch of chips that had fallen on the floor and been forgotten. And above me, I saw through the glass table well enough to spot three empty wine bottles and an almost empty overturned ice cream carton that had leaked onto the table.

A headache unlike anything I'd felt in years blazed to life, and I groaned at the memory of my night of binge-watching. Yeah, sure, I'd finally watched that show with the hottie everyone was always talking about. And yeah, maybe when I was halfway through my second bottle I'd started shouting, "I'll throw a coin to you, you hot fox you!" But no, I wasn't proud of myself.

I realized the phone was still ringing and groaned as I sat up and snatched it.

Seeing my little brother's name, I swiped the screen and meant to say, "Hello," but instead my voice trailed off as I said, "Hell--."

Well, that about summed things up, didn't it?

There was a pause on the other end of the line. "You okay, Emma?"

I crawled to the couch. "Yeah, never better."

"You sure? Because last night you called me. A lot."

I cringed and pressed a throw pillow to my face and screamed into it for a second, then dropped the pillow onto the chips. "Yeah? What did I say?"

He was quiet for a long minute, and I wondered what he was thinking. He couldn't exactly say I was too old for this. In my forty-two long years I'd managed to live a responsible life. I'd always done the right thing. I'd always made the smartest choices.

While Henry? I had no doubt he'd be dead if I wasn't constantly bailing him out.

"Are you and Rick getting a divorce?"

My stomach dropped. I hadn't actually said the words out loud, not to anyone. But I guess all I needed to do was get drunk for the first time since college, and who knew what I'd done?

I released a slow breath and let my hand fall back. It crunched, and I looked on the end table to find an open bag of chips. Unable to help myself, I reached in and stuffed some in my face. I was a mess. And if I was going to be a mess, then I might as well be a mess while I slid down screaming into all the carbs I'd denied myself for years.

"Yeah," I said, mouth full. "Rick was cheating on me with his secretary."

"With Bella? I thought you said that girl was like a daughter to him. Didn't he even help her pay for college?"

"He did. With money from my 401k. But I was a moron and really believed him when he said nothing was going on."

My brother cursed under his breath. "You okay?"

"Sure." I reached for another handful of chips. "I'm not going to help run his company anymore though. The company I've sunk years and years into. The company I made into a successful business when he was paying his employees with cash advances from his credit card." A laugh that didn't sound like my own exploded from my lips. "So there's that! There's that shining nugget of fun that I can toss in the air like confetti along with twenty years of marriage." Another slightly crazy laugh came, and this time I coughed out some chips.

"No offense, but you don't sound like you're doing well. Need me to come there?" There was legitimate concern in my brother's voice. And my brother wasn't exactly good with empathy, or even picking up on other people's emotions.

I swallowed the rest of my chips and slowly sat up. Around me, the living room was trashed, and the screen was paused on a view of my new celebrity crush sitting in what was supposed to be something like a hot tub. How many times had I replayed him in that hot tub last night? I cringed. Too many. Way too many. I think I was one more drink away from kissing the screen.

No more alcohol for me. Alcoholic drinks and I didn't mix well.

I sighed. "No, I don't need you to come here. I'll figure it out. I promise. I'll be okay."

"If you're sure." He sounded like he didn't believe me.

I stood and started gathering the party-size load of

empty bags of chips. Frowning, I looked around myself, then decided to stack it all on the box of pizza. A box that was empty too.

"So, Henry, what do you need?"

"Actually, uh, some stuff came up and--"

"How *much* do you need?"

"Maybe like five hundred."

I sighed. It wasn't exactly the best time to be giving away money, now that I was newly unemployed and had no idea what my life was going to be like. But Henry always came first. He was my only sibling, my little brother by five years, and he needed me.

"I'll send it over."

"Thanks, sis," he said, then hung up.

Henry was never good at saying goodbye, but then when he was younger a lot of people never thought he'd go on to get a job, have a relationship, or anything. It was a testament to how much my parents loved him that they got him into the right therapists and with the right teachers. Now it wasn't as obvious as when he was little that he was autisitic, but although he had his job and lived on his own in our parent's old house, he still had me handle things like the bills, setting up doctor's appointments, and all of those kinds of things. When I'd left our home town, it'd been the hardest thing either of us had to do since our parents died.

I swallowed the lump at the back of my throat as I remembered the night of the car crash. After all this time, the memories didn't hurt as much, but they still made my heart ache from the loss. Like the pain in my neck that was better now, but still twinged, still reminded me that Henry and I hadn't walked away from that crash without a scratch.

Grabbing an armful of trash, I managed to get out the front door. The garbage can was still at the curb, something

I was used to Rick taking care of, so I awkwardly made my way down to the street. The entire time I found myself glaring at the black bin. Rick had one chore around the house, *one*, but it still irritated me that now I had to do that. Now I had to do *everything*, because I no longer had a partner.

Stupid trashcan. And stupid trash human being.

I was about to awkwardly try to open the bin when a sound made me lift my head. My teeth grit together. The neighbor's kid loved to fly around the corner like it was his own personal mission in life to come up the hill of our street and go airborne. I'd talked to his parents more times than I could count, but they didn't care. Said something about being an internet "personality" and that his car videos always got a lot of likes.

I'd added them to my list of people who needed karma's big boot to kick their asses.

I was about to toss the trash in the can when I saw a woman starting to walk across the road just at the top of the hill. My heart dropped into my stomach. I knew that from the time I heard the idiot kid's car and him getting to the top of the hill was no time at all. Any minute he'd come flying at her.

"Hey!"

The older woman continued limping across the road.

"Hey," I shouted again, dropping the trash on the ground.

I didn't know what I was doing when I started running. I was sure the neighbors were going to look out of their windows at any second and see me racing along, barefoot, in stained pajamas, braless boobs flopping, but I couldn't shake the feeling that if I couldn't get there in time something bad was going to happen.

I'd nearly reached her when I heard the car's engine at the bottom of the hill. Everything inside of me said not to step into that street. Not to run right to the place I knew a car was about to be, but the woman was there. A woman who would die if I wasn't fast enough.

My hands stretched out as I saw a flash of the kid's car and I shoved the older woman, trying not to slow down as I did. Something hit my shoulder, hard, and then I was on the pavement panting, pain radiating through my arm as I stared at the early morning sky.

A groan exploded from my lips, but the squeal of tires drowned it out. I rolled onto my good side and saw the idiot kid's car, the mirror lying broken on the ground. His door opened. He stepped out, eyes wide, swore, and got back into his car and drove off.

"Little idiot is going to get a beating from karma when I--" I was still gasping for air as I tried to struggle to my feet.

"Karma will get him, don't you worry,"

I stiffened and looked in the direction of the voice.

The older woman stared down at me, and I was stunned into silence for a minute. She had a strange elegance about her, like royalty. Her hair was pure white and mostly concealed beneath a pale pink hat with a flower, and she wore a matching pink suit with a skirt. Her hands were folded over a cane, and she looked at me with amusement.

I climbed to my feet, gripping my shoulder, my teeth clenching together so I didn't cry out in pain. "Are you okay?"

She nodded. "But you're not okay."

"I think it's just dislocated," I said, but the truth was I had no idea. I just knew it hurt so much I was about to vomit. "I'm sure I'll be fine."

That smile of hers didn't change. "Your husband is an

asshole. You never have any fun. And you wish your life was completely different."

After a second, I realized my mouth was hanging open.

"Oh, and you're giving and kind, and threw yourself in front of a car for a stranger."

I forced my mouth to work. "How do-- how is--?"

"Not to worry. But believe me, karma's coming for that boy, and karma's coming for you."

I frowned and looked back in the direction the car had gone, then back to the lady. But she was gone.

Which was impossible.

Staggering off the road, I gave in to the heaving in my stomach and hurled into Mrs. Wilders's prized roses, wiped my mouth with the back of my hand, then headed for my house. I ignored the wine bottles scattered by the curb, the empty pizza box, bags of chips, and ice cream carton, and stumbled into my house, locking the door behind me. Breathing hard, I went to the couch and fell onto it.

Darkness swallowed me, but my last thought was that I was probably losing my mind. That there was never any old woman. That maybe there wasn't even a car.

I could handle losing my husband. I *couldn't* handle losing my mind.

2

EMMA

I woke up to hear pounding at my door. Blinking my eyes open, I hissed in a breath as my shoulder throbbed. Using my good hand, I pushed myself into a sitting position, and my stomach rolled from the wave of pain. It radiated through my chest and down my arm. The sudden urge to hurl again came over me and stars danced in front of my vision.

The pounding came again, and I stood, the ground tilting under me, and headed for the door. Before I knew what I was doing, I threw back the brand new locks and opened the door. On the other side, my ex-husband stood with his new girlfriend next to him. He looked ridiculous. He had obviously put plugs in his dark hair, and I could have sworn he had makeup and even eye-liner on. He was wearing skinny jeans and a shirt with a band logo on it, a band I happen to know he hated. The woman at his side was barely twenty, young enough to be his daughter, and she wore a cut-off shirt that exposed her belly button piercing and jeans that said Wet and Wild Woman along the side.

I blinked at them both.

It took my ex a long minute to speak, and then he launched into that irritating voice of his. "What the hell, Emma? What's going on? There's trash all over the front yard. You look like you slept in a dumpster. Is this some pathetic plan to try to win me back?"

My head rang with every word that left his thin lips. "*Win you back*? Win *you* back? Like some cheater who can't manage money is such a prize, Rick."

He flinched as I spoke.

His new girl tossed her hair over his shoulder. "*I* think he's a prize."

I couldn't help but smile. "But will you think he's such a prize when a few years from now he starts boning his new secretary?"

Her mouth dropped open.

"Close you mouth, sweetheart, you look stupid like that," I said, unable to help myself.

Rick stepped in front of her. "Leave her alone. I came to get my stuff, and then we're gone."

"Go ahead," I said. "I put everything you own in boxes in the garage." After letting the neighbor's new puppies urinate all over them, but I kept that to myself.

He gave a huff. "I was going to let the lawyers tell you, but since you continue acting like a bitch, I'll save them the trouble. If you think this divorce is going to break me, you have another thing coming. The house, the cars, the business, they're all in my name. And since you signed a prenup-"

"I never signed a prenup," I said, shocked.

"My lawyer would beg to differ. He's ready and willing to testify that he saw you sign the prenup we prepared a few weeks before we got married."

"Wait." My head spun. "Is your lawyer your *cousin*?"

He grinned. "The best lawyer in the state. And when we're done, you're going to have nothing."

The idiot beside him grabbed his arm. "You said there was jewelry?"

Something inside of me snapped. "You're not going to get away with this! I never signed a prenup, and I'll prove it. You were underwater on this house when I met you. I used my savings to buy the cars. And that business is going to sink without me, so don't even pretend to try to take credit for my hard work." And then I turned to the woman. "The jewelry in this house is mine. Take that garbage man, but stay away from my diamonds."

She pouted. Like a two-year-old.

"I want my stuff," he said, his voice cold.

I opened the door wider, biting down on the cry of pain that the movement caused in my shoulder. He strode past me, his dog at his heels, and they both headed for the door that led to the garage. I didn't take a breath until the garage door slammed and I heard the big door opening that led to the outside.

Then, tears pricked my eyes. Not because of the two idiots. Because of my arm.

I went to the back door and opened it, using my free hand to dab at my eyes. Then I clenched my teeth together to keep from crying out as I walked to the bench in my garden and collapsed onto it. Feeling ridiculous, I tried to wipe away every tear before it could fall. I should be able to handle this, all of this, so why was it so hard?

"Karma."

I jumped a little at the sound and looked around, but no one was there.

"Karma."

I looked toward the sound, then slowly picked out the

shape of a toad sitting by the edge of the little pond in my backyard. I was shaking for some reason. Maybe because my ex and his new lover were digging through my garage. Maybe because I was pretty sure I would pass out from the pain before I could make it to Urgent Care. Or maybe because I could swear the toad kept saying the word "karma," but I couldn't be sure.

Sometime later, the door to the backyard opened. I didn't bother turning around; I just kept staring at the toad. They came and stood in front of me, blocking my view of the toad, and I slowly looked up. I was shocked by just how pleased they both looked with themselves. And for the first time it really hit me that after betraying me, after leaving me after twenty years of marriage, neither of these people felt the least bit remorseful.

They were just terrible people.

I didn't know what I was about to do, but suddenly something caught the light. I stood slowly to find that she, this bitch child who was banging my piece of shit husband, was wearing my mother's necklace. The locket with her image inside, and easily the most important thing I own.

"My mother's locket." Horror rose inside me. Pure shock that they could possibly be this cruel.

My ex shrugged. "I own everything in this house anyway."

The fuck he did.

Anger like nothing I'd ever felt in my life coursed through me. Breathing hard, I tried to calm myself, but it was as if white hot fire filled my lungs and the air warmed around me like the moment before a volcanic explosion. I even imagined the ground starting to shake. It had to be in my head, but it was all I could do to keep from clawing at this bitch with my good hand. I couldn't attack her, though, because if she fought back I'd pass out from the pain in my arm.

Lifting my good hand I pointed at them both. "Karma's going to get you!" And I knew I sounded a little crazy, but then the toad on the ground croaked again, and I said the first thing that came to mind. "You—you're both freaking toads!"

From one blink of the eye to the next, they were gone.

I stood, confused, when I heard a croak and slowly lowered my eyes. There, where they were standing, were two toads, and their clothes beneath them in piles. And one of the toads had my mother's necklace lying over it.

Slowly, I knelt down and picked up the locket.

The toads gave me sad croaks as I blinked back down at them, and my legs shook as I slowly stood back up. *Did I just turn them into toads?* That was not possible. This was like the old lady and the car. I was having some kind of breakdown. I was losing my mind.

I needed to get out of here. I raced inside and ignored the messy living room. Going to my room, I used one hand to pick out a shirt, pants, and a bra, and I dressed one-handed, finally giving in to the pain and screaming when I had to get my arm into the shirt. Then, fully dressed, I grabbed my keys and headed out the front door.

There, parked in my driveway, was my ex's car.

My heart raced. I moved through the backyard like I was in a nightmare. The toads weren't on the piles of clothes anymore, but I knelt down and found my ex's wallet and keys in the pants.

If this was some sort of breakdown, it was a good one.

And if I really just turned them into toads, I needed to hide the evidence. I'd seen way too many detective shows. If they turned up missing, I was the first person anyone would look into. And if the police found their clothes and car here, I was in trouble.

I didn't know what I was doing when I grabbed their stuff with my good hand and ran back out front, but I threw their clothes into the passenger seat and put the keys in the ignition. The back seats were full of my ex's stuff, and I saw my jewelry box on the floor.

Gritting my teeth, I put the car in reverse and pulled out of my driveway. I was going to toss the clothes in a random dumpster, then leave the car at his new apartment complex. When I was done, I'd take a cab to the hospital near me and get my shoulder fixed.

Oh, and I was going to take back my jewelry box.

After that, I had no idea. But I had to figure out what the heck was going on.

And get out of town until I got a grip. Fortunately for me, I knew just where I was going to go.

Home.

3

EMMA

Mystic Hollow was the perfect little town, and as I drove down the coast, windows rolled down, I felt another wave of anger at my ex. I should've never left this town. The salty water, the white beaches, even the woods, they were all a part of me. I had all of my best memories in this place.

It'd never stopped feeling like home.

But he hadn't wanted to move here. So, we didn't. I resented him for that, but I resented myself even more. Because with each day that had passed since the Day of Strangeness, I'd started to realize how many times I'd given into Rick.

I'd given in and given in until I was living a life I wasn't happy in. And that was just as much on me as it was on him.

I shifted my shoulder in the brace, and took the next one-handed curve in the road slowly. The urgent care doctors had said I'd probably bruised my bones, but they'd fixed the dislocated shoulder, so it wasn't nearly as painful as before. Not that you'd know it from the gnarly bruise that had spread over my painfully white skin. Still, I was hurting as I came to this last stretch of the drive. A couple days in a car was already hard on my bum, back, and neck. The shoulder just added a whole other *fun* element to being crammed into a car all night.

Slowing down even more, I reached the road with all of the beautiful beach houses spread out, facing the ocean. If I stayed on this path, I'd come to the town of Mystic Hollow, and if I kept going, I'd find woods in every direction. This place was isolated.

Which was exactly what I needed.

I turned another curve and saw the spot where the road broke off. One way led to the quiet street with beach houses, and the other went into town. I took the quiet road, watching the ocean waves between the houses and tilting my face up to feel the sunlight on it. My gaze pulled from the ocean, and I looked ahead, waiting to catch sight of our house. But when it came into view, I was a little surprised. It was in rougher shape than I remembered.

Pulling into the driveway, I killed the engine and climbed out. Outside, the scent of the ocean was even stronger, and the sound of the waves hitting the shore was like the sweetest music. Muscles I didn't know were clenched relaxed, and I walked slowly to the porch.

My brother rose from one of the two rocking chairs, and I froze. Was he taller than I remembered? Henry was always so tall and so thin. His dark hair, the same almost-black brown shade as my own, was still left long, like when he was a boy. And yet, he'd filled out a little. He even had some softness around his stomach.

I smiled. "Henry!"

He grinned and walked out to meet me. When we reached each other, he awkwardly leaned in and gave me a loose hug before he pulled back. "Welcome home."

"It looks the same," I said.

He shrugged.

"Want to help me bring my bags in?"

He nodded, and we went to the car and started unloading it. "What happened to your arm?"

"Just a car accident."

He stood to his full height, loaded with my bags, and I closed the door. We went back up the path, climbed the patio stairs, and headed inside. The big living room, filled with huge floor-to-ceiling windows, made me catch my breath. I wandered to the windows and pressed a hand to the glass, staring out at the wild waters. How many times had I laid by these windows and read as a child? How many times did I sit out on that beach and let the waves wash over me?

"Do you want to go in your old room or mom's and dad's?"

I stiffened and looked back at him. "You're not in the master?"

He shook his head.

"I guess—I guess their room."

He nodded and took off down the hall.

I followed after him, through the big open kitchen, and passed my old bedroom, the bathroom we shared, and his room, before coming to the last room. The door was open, but I entered hesitantly. After my parents had died, we'd stayed in this house. After a time, I'd redone this room, erasing most of the memories that hurt to remember, but still it felt weird to be in here. He set the bags down on the bed and turned back to me.

"My girlfriend and I have plans to play War Guild online."

I grinned. "So things are still going well with you and Alice?"

He nodded. "She's my girlfriend."

"Okay," I said. "I'm fine. You go have fun."

He left, not looking back, and I couldn't help but smile. He and Alice had been dating for ten years. She still lived with her parents. He still lived here. They both just liked their space, according to him, and they were both happy with things exactly the way they were. It was kind of strange to me. Everything about their relationship was unconventional. They just did what made them happy, and yet, I was the one getting a divorce.

Maybe this time around I should just try to be happy too.

I slipped my phone from my pocket and sent Travis a quick text letting him know I'd made it to Mystic Hollow without any issues. He might have only just started college, but he had an old soul, and ever since Rick's cheating had been outed, he'd worried about me like he was the mom instead of me.

After a few minutes, I got a thumbs up back.

So articulate.

Touching my mother's locket, I tried not to think about the toads in my garden, the clothes tossed behind a fast food restaurant not far from my house, or the car that I'd parked in his spot in his new apartment complex; or at least in the spot I thought was his. It wasn't like I murdered them. It wasn't like I did anything.

But then again, I thought I turned them into toads, so who knew what I'd really done?

I tossed the dusty sheets and blankets in the wash, unpacked, and went to get a snack. Every piece of food in the fridge was labeled with Henry's name, all still on his half of the fridge, just like it had been when it was the two of us living together. I grinned and decided that it'd be better just to head to the store.

Well, it would have been if I wasn't exhausted from driving most of the day with a braced shoulder.

Take-out it was. The store could wait until tomorrow. It wasn't like I needed breakfast to survive, and the take-out would get me through lunch if I managed to sleep in.

Now the big question. Pizza or burgers?

That may have been the big question, but the real question was whether or not I'd be able to stay awake long enough to actually eat it. I hadn't realized how late it was or how tired I was.

OUTSIDE ONCE MORE, I took a deep breath of the late morning air, letting the salty scent fill my lungs before I drove the relaxing path to the closest store in town. There were only a few spots out front, but I managed to catch someone backing out. I turned on my blinker and waited, but when they pulled out, another car swooped in and took the spot.

My mouth dropped open. I unrolled my other window and shouted, "I was waiting for that spot!"

A lady with a bad perm turned around and grinned. "You don't own a parking spot."

When she whirled away from me, I glared and narrowed my eyes.

Suddenly, a loud sound, followed by three more big pops, made me jump. The woman turned back around, and we both stared at her four flat tires. Her jaw dropped. My jaw dropped. I stepped on the gas and decided to head for the other store in town.

I was shaking a little when I reached the store a few minutes later and parked. Tires pop all the time. Right? It wasn't because I was glaring at her. It wasn't anything I did. No one could possibly blame me for it.

Grabbing my purse, I awkwardly put it over one shoulder and headed inside. Pushing the darn cart ended up being harder than I thought as I tried to shop and do it one-handed. As I tried to push it unevenly through the people leaving, I ran into one person, who cast me a dirty look, and then another. When I turned to apologize to the second person, the front of my cart hit a pile of cans, and suddenly they were raining down on the ground like gunfire going off.

When the last can rolled and stopped in front of my cart, I felt every eye in the place on me. Wincing, cheeks burning hot, I started trying to pick up the cans. Which was another thing that was surprisingly hard to do one-handed.

"You need some help?"

The man's voice was deep and filled with amusement. Even before I looked up I was preparing myself for someone hot, but when my eyes met his deep green eyes, I wasn't ready for what I saw. Since becoming single, I'd found that most of the men I saw out and about were either way too young for me, happily married, or looked like they were my ex. But this man? He was *handsome*, especially with his auburn hair that had grey peppered at his temples, and a slight scruff of beard with the same grey peppered in it. He was probably my age, but he didn't have the same signs of flab that I had at my arms and belly, the flab I couldn't seem to get rid of. Instead, he had big arms and the kind of hard chest and trim waist that made my mouth water.

"You must be married."

The second the words left my lips, I winced and looked down at the cans, continuing to put them flat on their bottom, in a sad pile.

I heard him laugh, and he had the sexiest laugh I'd ever heard. "Actually, no."

And then he knelt down beside me and started to add to my stack. Our hands brushed once, and I knew I had to be imagining the electricity that seemed to course between us.

"I'm a widower," he said. "Nearly ten years now."

Oh, damn. But I couldn't help but wish Rick had died. Was that too mean of me?

Meh, I didn't care even if it was. He was a dick.

"I'm Daniel," he said. "Daniel Arthur. I'd shake your hand but you only seem to have one to use at the moment."

I laughed and looked at him again. "Oh, I know you. You went to Mystic Hollow High, right?"

He grinned and picked up four cans in one hand with ease.

Big hands, big heart. Yeah. Heart. That was the expression.

"I did. Graduated in, ah." He grinned guiltily. "I'd rather not say."

I snorted. "I know how that feels. I'm Emma. Emma Pierce. I used to be Emma Foxx, before I got married."

"You're married?" he asked, and I might've imagined the shock and disappointment in his voice.

Why was I so stupid? Man, I sucked at being single.

"Sort of?"

Daniel grabbed the last few cans and I tried to rise as gracefully as possible. Not one foot at a time, grasping the side of the buggy like I wanted to. When I was a teenager, I could stand up from sitting cross-legged on the floor without uncrossing my legs. I could just stand. Just like that.

But oh, no. Not now. "Sort of, as in I'm in the middle of a divorce. To a toad."

I swallowed a panicked laugh cause I was literally married to a toad. I thought.

This time, I glanced at him through my lashes but couldn't read anything from his expression. I'd definitely imagined him being disappointed that I was married. This wasn't one of those perfect moments in movies where I meet the stud I was always supposed to be with. This was real life, and he was just being nice to a woman with an arm in a sling. That was it.

"Let me push that for you," Daniel offered.

I nodded, and we started through the store together. It took a surprising amount of effort not to look at him, so I focused on everything I knew about him from long ago. Old memories from high school came pouring back like no time at all had passed. And there was Daniel in the heart of so many memories. Cute Daniel, who had no idea I even existed.

Now that I recognized him, it made sense that I thought he was hot. I'd had a massive unrequited crush on him in high school. "Thank you. That's so kind." He picked an aisle and I grabbed all sorts of things, knowing my brother's tics. I wouldn't be able to use any of the food he had in the house. "So, what else have you been up to since high school?" I asked as I grabbed a package of flour.

"Well, I was the sheriff of Mystic Hollow until my wife died, then I retired. I help with the youth programs in town now."

"That's so nice. I mean, not the part about your wife dying, but the other stuff," I said, wanting to smack myself upside the head for putting my foot in my mouth again, even though I genuinely meant it. Early retirement, though. We were hardly at a retiring age, and if his wife had died a decade before, he would've been in his thirties.

"I still work part time." He looked at the cereal, then selected a sugary brand and put it in the child-basket at the front of the cart. "Help out where I can."

There was a story there, but he was helping me push my buggy so I didn't pry. "How about you?" he asked.

"Um, I'm getting a divorce, so I came back home for the moment to escape the stress of it. That's about all, at the moment. I helped run my husband's company and turn it into a success, so I may look for something in management? I'm not sure."

His eyes almost seemed to twinkle under the fluorescent lights. "Well, I have no doubt you'll figure it out. You always had a good head on your shoulders."

I stiffened. Did he remember me? There was no way. He was captain of the football team, and I was learning to knit with my friends on the weekends, watching only romance movies.

His phone beeped, and he pulled it out of his pocket and frowned at it.

"Problem?" I asked.

His gaze met mine. "Just something I need to take care of."

"Well, I can manage my cart now, as long as I stay away from all the giant piles of cans."

He laughed. "You sure?"

I nodded.

He grinned and grabbed his cereal, then hesitated. "You don't need me to grab anything heavy for you before I go?"

I couldn't take my gaze off of his teeth. They were

perfectly white, and the front one had the tiniest chip in it. "No," I said dreamily. "I'm good, but thank you so much."

He nodded at me again. "It was good running into you. I'm sure I'll see you around." He walked toward the registers since we'd reached the front of the aisle. Since I wasn't finished, I went on around to the next aisle. As I moved down it, I looked back to find him standing at the register but staring at me.

I quickened my steps to get out of sight.

Holy hot flash. I wasn't in menopause yet, but I was having a hot flash right now.

Geez. Daniel Arthur was everything Rick wasn't. Maybe I was crazy, but having an almost random guy help me without needing to be asked felt like a treat. Rick had always been like a child I had to care for. Constantly needing attention. Whining that he couldn't eat if I didn't cook. Whining when he didn't like what I *did* cook.

Man, why had I put up with it?

I thought of Daniel again. I bet he was never like that with his wife. He seemed like the kind of man who genuinely loved other people more than himself.

Or maybe I was just romanticizing the first man I'd felt anything for in years. That was probably it.

I grabbed some snacks off the shelf and willed myself not to think of Daniel again. Right now my job was to pull myself and my life together again, not lust after guys I didn't even know. My twenties and thirties were long gone. Forty-year-old me would not make the same mistakes as before.

Still, I smiled when I thought of Daniel.

4

EMMA

An employee pushed the cart out to my car and loaded the bags. If only I could've taken him home with me to do the same, but Mystic Hollow was way too small to have grocery delivery. We were lucky to have two grocery stores.

As I pulled out of the parking lot, my car beeped at me. I looked down and the needle for the gas gauge was perilously close to the edge of the red line. Dang it. Of course I needed gas, but for some reason, it was the last thing I wanted to do in life. Getting out of the car. Pumping. Making awkward conversation with the person who inevitably pulled up on the other side of the pump. Smelling like gas for hours afterward. I wanted nothing to do with it. At least not right now.

Adulting was irritating sometimes. Scratch that. All the time.

I pulled into the gas station in town near my old high school, which was also on the way home. It hadn't changed a bit since I was last here. There were even teenagers still hanging out on the wall to one side of the building with big sodas and skateboards. But now, instead of there being open lots on both sides, there was a little shopping center to the right that I instantly liked. It consisted of a collection of little stores with dark faux-thatched roofs, with robin's egg blue painted walls, which only looked even brighter when combined with the white shutters and white doors. It had the same cozy feel as most of the places here. The only difference was that these stores had been built in the last ten years. I was glad whoever designed them had kept the small town feel to them. None of them were even over a single story in height. Nothing to obscure the skyline.

One of the stores was a coffee shop with a big sign that said Cafe Mama. Just the sight of the place had my mouth watering. If I needed anything in this world, it was coffee. I jittered up and down on my toes so much as I pumped the gas that I probably looked like some kind of weirdo, then I quickly moved the car and parked in front of the coffee shop.

As soon as I walked in the door, the scent of roasted coffee and sweet treats hit me, along with the fact that I saw someone I knew. Not too surprising for a town this small, but what was surprising was that she was one of the only people I was unbelievably happy to be running into, even if it meant delaying my coffee addiction.

I froze, not wanting to interrupt as she helped a woman with a walker get her coffee and situate it in a special carrying case that hooked onto the front bar of her walker before helping her sit in one of the plush, overstuffed armchairs. I stood there like I'd been cemented to the spot and let my gaze run over her. Beth was as easily recognizable now as she had been then. She was just under five feet tall, which meant pretty much everyone in town towered over her. Her blonde hair had been left long, and it was just as thick and luxurious as it had been in high school, something I had always envied and did all over again the moment I saw her. She had the same curvy body, and the same style. She wore light wash jeans and a white flowy top with embroidered flowers on it. The only thing that was really different about her were the lines on her face and the bold shade of pink lipstick.

Staring at her was like stepping back into time. Did she have the same sweet personality she used to, or had time warped that as well?

"Beth?"

She had just straightened from helping the older woman sit when her gaze fell on me and her eyes widened. I could tell she was looking at me the same way I'd looked at her as she stared from my feet slowly up to my face. It was hard not to squirm. Not to wonder if she was thinking how much thinner I had been back then, or how I hadn't needed a special bra to keep my boobs looking decently perky. And could she tell my hair was dyed instead of natural now.

When her face lit up, some of the tension eased inside of me. "Emma! I didn't know you were visiting."

I was ashamed of how long it had been since I came home to visit. My brother had driven out to see me a few times, but it had been too many years since I came home. Still, it was no excuse for not keeping in touch with the people who had mattered to me the most.

I forced a smile. How do you tell people that you have nowhere else to go? That you've moved back into your parents place because your husband was a cheating asshole and might now be a toad? "Yeah, I decided spur of the moment to come for an extended stay."

She walked away from the door and pulled me in for a hug. "Well, come have a cup of coffee."

Even in high school, I'd loved my coffee. So, we walked through the cafe together, even though she already had a cup. I ordered their biggest size and tried not to to tap my fingers while I watched her pour the sweet liquid of life. Then I paid the cashier, gave her a tip, and we headed outside.

"Do you still own the detective agency?" I asked, hoping I was remembering correctly.

She nodded. "Just two shops down. Have time for a sit down?"

I only had a few cold things in my groceries and it was a fairly cool day. They could wait. The worst I'd get was some melted ice cream, and even that was iffy. "Sure. Let's catch up."

We passed a shop full of what looked like a tea store, lots of jars of leaves on the shelves and some fancy-schmancy tea pots in the window, then came to stop in front of a building with the words, "Private Psych," on the front door. There were big picture windows that looked out on the parking lot, the sidewalk lined by trees, and the main city road. She unlocked the door and we stepped into the strangest building I'd ever been in. The front had a sitting area with comfortable, worn-looking couches that were a cream color, a coffee table that was all dark wood and glass, matching end tables, and lamps with stained glass enclosures that were made up of different animals. After the neat sitting area, there were shelves covering the walls. Most were filled with books, especially toward the top and bottom, but there was also a mouse cage on one of the middle shelves, and a lamp sitting over a cage with a lizard or gecko or something that reminded me of those car insurance commercials. The back wall had more books, but also cat climbing trees that went from floor to ceiling with cat-sized walkways between them, where several cats snoozed. There was a big desk covered in papers, and near it an open bird platform with something that looked like a crow sleeping.

And yet, as crazy as the room was, it kind of fit Beth's personality perfectly.

Trailing my hands over the dark velvet-like fur of a tabby cat snoozing in a ray of sunshine, I settled into one of Beth's oversized chairs in front of her desk and sipped my coffee.

We didn't have a chance to really start talking when the soft chime over her door started tinkling. A woman barged in carrying a bright pink smoothie, and slammed the door behind her. The cat that had just been sleeping so peacefully jumped up and hissed before streaking out of the room to somewhere past beaded curtains in the back.

"You were supposed to prove he's a cheating bastard!" she yelled.

Beth took a deep breath and stood before walking toward the woman. "April, what is this? I did. I got the information you requested."

"I talked to my husband and he denied everything. You made it all up."

Beth looked at the woman like she was totally nuts. "April, I gave you pictures. There was no doubt that your husband was a cheater."

"You're a fraud, Beth Ari! A fraud and a shyster!"

Beth shrugged. "It's not my fault if you don't want to believe the truth."

The woman froze and her chin rose. "You're just angry because Roger left you. Trying to ruin everyone else's relationships because yours didn't work. Oh, he had so many promises. Didn't he? But we all knew he was with her the whole time. It seems you can figure out any secret, except the secrets in your own house, huh?"

Beth's normally warm toned skin went absolutely pale as all the blood seemed to drain from her face. The worst part was that she didn't say a word, which was completely unlike her.

The woman grinned in a way that said she knew her words had hit their mark before she spun on her heel and headed for the door.

Rage filled me. Even if none of what the woman said was true, which I seriously doubted, it was a cruel thing to say. Beth was one of the kindest people I'd ever met. She didn't deserve to be hurt like that.

I eyed the woman's back, and said loudly enough for just Beth and I to hear, "Sounds like she deserves a big dose of Karma."

As soon as the words left my mouth, the woman tripped on thin air. The top of her smoothie popped open and the pink sludge crashed against her chest and poured all over her front.

A snort erupted from my mouth before I could control myself. She turned, like she was covered in blood instead of smoothie, her mouth hanging open like a fish. She made a little sound like a dog's squeaky toy.

"Well! Aren't you two going to do anything?" Her face turned pinker than her spilled smoothie.

Unable to help myself, I shrugged. "Must have been those invisible ninjas."

I couldn't have stopped the grin that covered my face even if I wanted to, so I embraced it and rose, then snagged one single tissue out of the box on Beth's desk. I walked toward her, but instead of stopping and offering her the tissue, insult though it would be, I pulled the door open and held it for her.

Her mouth finally snapped closed. "I hope you both go

to hell!" She stormed toward the door I was holding open, chunks of smoothie dripping off her chest and landing on her legs as she went, as though it was some weird, perfectly choreographed disaster.

I gave her a little wave with the tissue. "And make sure you watch out for those invisible ninjas!"

Her eyes flashed with rage, and she rushed out the door. Once she was outside, I watched her finally grimace at the state of her clothes as she moved along, and couldn't help but laugh. That pink color was never going to come out of her white running top and matching yoga pants.

Beth walked over and peered down at the floor. "I don't know how this is possible, but she didn't spill a single drop of that smoothie."

My breathing suddenly froze. Oh no, not again.

Beth looked at me in wonder, and I tried not to look too guilty. I had an idea of how it was possible, but I hoped it wasn't written all over my face. I mean, I didn't even want to believe it myself, but I was beginning to think I had something to do with these karmic things happening.

Beth looked at me, then back at the spot on the floor where smoothie should've been splattered. "Did you do that?"

"M-me?" I stuttered. "I wasn't even near her."

Beth made a humming sound as she turned and walked back to her desk, shooing another cat out of the way as she sat back down, and I returned to the big chair in front of her, feeling nervous. "I know damn well you were human when you left Mystic Hollow, so you can't be a shifter or a vampire. Are you some sort of witch that can hide your powers?"

What in the world was she talking about?

"No, I didn't do that. I mean, I've had some freaky things

happen over the past few days, but are you really talking about vampires and shifters?"

Beth leaned in closer and stared directly into my eyes as though she could find the truth within them, which made me want to look away, but I couldn't. Then she held her hands in front of me, her palms facing me like she wanted me to give her a high five, before moving them up and down and around in circles, bracelets jangling as she went. I looked at them with my eyebrows furrowed and my back pressed into the back of the chair.

"What are you doing?" I squinted at her. Beth had always been quirky, but this was new.

"I'm reading your aura," she said. "But it's not easy."

"Beth."

She ignored me.

"*Beth*!" I yelled.

She jerked her hands back and gave me a startled look. "Why are you yelling?"

"Because you're talking about reading my aura, whatever that even means, and vampires and shifters. What the hell is going on?"

She laughed, her eyes crinkling at the edges as she looked around. "Hey, Marble!"

A cat, which appeared to be aptly named, as she was a calico with marbled white, brown, and orange fur, trotted over. "Yeah?"

I nearly fell off the chair. My head spun.

"Say hi to Emma," Beth said to the cat. She said that *to* the cat.

"Hi, Emma." Marble looked me over in that haughty way only cats can manage. "She might pass out."

Then Marble picked up one of her front paws and licked it before walking back across the front of the office and settling into the beam of sunshine that the dark tabby had been in earlier.

"She just talked to me," I whispered. "That cat."

Beth leaned forward. "Are you telling me you really don't know?"

"That cats can talk?"

"Well, yeah."

I shook my head. "Can they talk to everyone? Is that cat a special talking cat?"

Beth shook her head. "Sorry, no, it's my powers. I can talk to cats, well animals in general, and they can talk to humans when I'm in the immediate vicinity. It's my special witch Zoolingualism."

It was like something in my brain burnt out, leaving nothing but smoke behind.

"I turned my ex-husband and his little bitch into toads," I whispered.

Beth's jaw dropped. "How in the world did you do that?"

I had no idea. "I think, if I'm not totally nuts and all this stuff really happened, I did it because I saved a little old lady from being hit by a car."

Recognition dawned over her face. "Oh. Okay. Has stuff like what just happened been happening?"

My brain was still blinking like an empty word document waiting for someone to fill it, but that didn't stop my mouth from working without my consent. "Someone cut me off in traffic and all their tires simultaneously and suddenly popped."

Beth nodded sagely. "Yep. Hang on."

She jumped up and hurried through the office into a back room, but returned quickly with a book in hand. She began scanning the text, occasionally licking her finger so she could move through the book faster, until she found the page she was looking for. "Here. I thought so. Wow. This is amazing. It's so rare."

She turned the book toward me and there was a picture of the old woman drawn on the page. Not just any old woman. The exact old woman I'd seen. A chill rippled down my spine. "That's her," I whispered. "The woman I saved from the car."

Beth looked at me, her blue eyes wide and sparking with amazement. "You've become karma."

"Karma?" I repeated, frowning.

She nodded and picked up her phone and started texting. "I think we're going to need some help."

"I think I might be losing my mind," I whispered.

She grinned over her phone. "Oh, just pretend you're Alice, I'm friends with the Cheshire cat, and you can come join us at our tea party. I swear life won't be boring again."

I didn't know what the heck to say. If I was Alice, I'd definitely fallen into a world that was both crazy and exciting.

Or maybe I was just crazy.

5

EMMA

A few minutes passed while Beth continued to send texts, and I scanned over the book about karma. It seemed to be describing a magical woman capable of giving people exactly what they deserved, good or bad. And yet, it didn't make sense. I'd seen the woman in the picture. She wasn't some witch with a wand, or a fairy with wings, she was just an older woman, a woman who would've been killed had I not jumped in the way.

So what did this have to do with me, or the strange talking cat?

The bell over Beth's door rang, the soft sound barely registering in the back of my panicked mind as someone walked in the front door. Beth's phone rang at the same time, and she apologized, then grabbed it off her desk. I sat back and stared at that damn cat that just talked to me. I couldn't bring myself to turn and see if smoothie-lady was back. Not after the world seemed to have come off its axis.

"Carol," Beth called when her eyes darted from me to check on who had entered. I jerked upright and turned to see another old friend walking toward us.

Her light brown hair was threaded with grey and her blue eyes were tired with bags underneath. Not that I was one to judge. Bags under your eyes was the new thing, right? Who needed some expensive designer bag when I could have my very own racoon eyes? Okay, *maybe* not, but I kind of saw it as a requirement now for my friends. No bags? No friendship. Sorry, twenty-something year old. Perky breasts and a body that doesn't ache are just not *cool* anymore.

Now my stylish shoulder brace? That was my own *personal* thing. My friends didn't need to look like broken dolls to hang out with this cool lady.

Shut up, I told myself, taking a deep breath. I was just nervous. I'd known I'd be running into old friends in this town, but I hadn't prepared to see so many my first day. I hadn't even had time to try to make myself look like my world hadn't recently come crumbling down.

Carol didn't seem to realize who I was at first, which gave me time to take in all the little ways she'd changed since I'd last seen her, and all the ways she hadn't.

Her outfit was just as quirky as her outfits had been in high school. Carol had always marched to the beat of her own drum, sometimes literally, at least when she'd tried to join the marching band. Needless to say, that hadn't lasted long when the conductor realized she had no rhythm but loved to bang her drum as loud as humanly possible.

It may have irritated the marching band, but it made me love her even more. She was brave and fierce in ways I always wanted to be. And I was glad to see that, at least on the surface, that wild soul of hers was still there.

The long skirt she was wearing hit mid-calf and was covered in cocks. No, not *that* kind. Roosters, in black and white with pops of red, in all different positions covered it. This was paired with black and white houndstooth sky-high shoes and a black and white plaid top. The kicker was the green army or utility jacket, though. It looked more than a little out of place with the flowing skirt, heels, and blousy top. The glasses that perched on her nose had bright red frames which matched the bright red lipstick she wore.

Carol was never one to shy away from loud patterns or bright colors. It was comforting to see that was still true too.

"Hello," Beth crooned into the phone behind me. "Yes, one sec." She covered the mouthpiece. "I have to take this. Carol, watch her. She just found out about the supernatural world. Be gentle."

Carol's eyes widened, nearly filling the space inside the red frames. "Ohhh, that's juicy." She plopped down in the chair across from me. I watched as she pulled out her knitting and picked up her needles, hooking the glittery purple yarn over her finger just so. "Tell me about it?" But when her gaze fell on me, her eyes widened. "Emma? Emma, is it really you?"

I forced a smile. "In the flesh."

"And you finally know about the supernatural world?" She seemed even more excited.

"I thought—I thought Beth might have texted you about it?"

She sighed and waved her hand. "I hate phones. I was just heading here anyway. So, you said you know about the supernatural world now? How?"

I didn't know where to begin. "Yeah. The cat talked to me," I whispered. Dread filled my stomach at the idea of this being some kind of elaborate prank, or some inside joke between the two of them. Clearly Carol was comfortable with Beth if she just came in and knit.

"Oh, yeah, of course. That's Beth's specialty. It's such a fun power and can really help out. She helped the police solve a couple of crimes after letting the household pets whisper in her ear, I'll tell ya." Carol nodded approvingly, briefly glancing at our friend with admiration.

"I had no idea any of this existed."

She winked. "I know. High school would've been a lot more fun if we hadn't had to be careful about saying or doing the wrong thing in front of our very human friend."

I sit back in my chair. In high school, I sometimes felt left out in our friend group. I'd always thought it was a normal teen thing, but what if I was wrong? So many moments from our past came back to me, and it's like they've taken on a whole new light.

"Homecoming dance when you guys didn't go shopping for a dress with me?"

She shrugged. "We had our own dresses magicked."

Suddenly, my gaze snapped from her face to her knitting needles. They clicked and they clacked, but once Carol had set up the needles and yarn she'd withdrawn her hands. In fact, her hands were folded in her lap and her gaze was on me.

"Your needles are knitting on their own." My voice sounded strange to my own ears, like it had risen an octave without my permission.

"Indeed they are." She paused and when I didn't immediately reply, she added, "I've been keeping an eye on your brother and girlfriend."

I nodded. "I know. I appreciate it." She'd emailed me a few times if she'd noticed anything she thought I should look into.

"I see them as my kids, in a way. His girlfriend is in my fabric shop quite a lot."

We had kept in touch, but only for the big stuff. I knew she had a fabric store, Yards and Yarns, where she sold everything to do with sewing, knitting, crocheting, anything textile based. There wasn't a lot I knew about the actual shop or how it came into being, though. So I asked, "How's the store doing?" After all, my parents had raised me to be polite. Apparently that still stuck with me, even through my friends outing themselves as having supernatural powers.

Or maybe I just needed something normal to cling to so my mind didn't explode.

"Oh, it's good. People are always trying to knit up here or teach themselves how to sew. It keeps me busy." She'd dreamed of opening this store all throughout high school and I was so happy for her that she was living her dream. A tiny part of me was jealous. I'd done everything I thought I was supposed to and got stuck with a shitty now ex-husband and the loss of my business and home. Although maybe the business would be mine again since he was a toad. Hell, I didn't even know if him being a toad was permanent. What if he popped back up and suddenly claimed everything as his again and just had a penchant for eating flies?

I realized I'd fallen silent so I said, "I think she sees it as a safe place. It's one of the few places she doesn't mind going. Henry and Alice generally spend time together at his home or hers, or more frequently on the internet playing games together. Neither of them go out a lot." As I spoke, my mind raced a mile a minute, thinking about all the things I'd learned in just the last five minutes. "Magic is real," I whispered.

"Indeed." Carol twiddled with the yarn, and it changed color, going from a sparkly purple to a peacock teal to a bright golden yellow until finally she settled on a lavender color. Once she was satisfied, she tapped the needles and they took over again. "Do you have questions?"

"Uh," I stuttered, unsure what to ask first as I was still

having trouble keeping my gaze from bouncing back and forth between the talking cat and the color changing yarn. Magic was real. I'd just seen two very real examples, which only became stronger when I added in everything else I'd been writing off as weird over the last few days. Finally I blurted, "Yes, actually. What does it mean that I'm Karma? Beth said it's rare and unusual, but that I'm Karma and showed me that book of an old woman I saved from being hit by a car back home. Well, what was my home anyway."

Carol's eyebrows raised high on her forehead, well passed the edge of her glasses. "Wow. That's pretty cool. Karma, huh? I thought that was a legend." She sucked in a deep breath and adjusted the yarn again, switching the color back to the sparkly purple it had been originally. "Well, most magic works essentially the same. You can learn to control most of it, but chances are when someone needs some karma near you, your powers will work whether you want them to or not."

"So say for instance a woman got a smoothie spilled down her top. I caused that even though I didn't mean to?"

Carol snorted and pushed her glasses up on her nose. "You did that, did you?"

"I think so?"

"She must have had a reason to deserve karma to smack her on the ass." When she paused, I nodded. "Then that was just your powers doing what they are going to do. Magic is nothing to be trifled with. Learn how to control your power and you'll be able to at least subdue the effects even if you can't halt them altogether."

My brain rolled the ideas around as though they were a grain of sand and I was an oyster who was trying to protect itself from the offending thought. It wasn't going to work though. Something in me had awoken now that I knew magic was real, and it wasn't going back to sleep any time soon. Besides, I had a feeling that this was just the beginning.

And that maybe magic was exactly what I needed in my life right now.

EMMA

As I gaped at Carol as her knitting project grew longer, the thought of my shiny new powers always expressing themselves whether I wanted them to or not filling my mind, another blast-from-the-past voice interrupted us.

"Emma!" The call of my name had me jolting in my seat, scared that someone would know what we were just talking about, or see Carol's knitting needles going by themselves, or even one of the cats carrying on a conversation.

As soon as the voice registered though, all my fear disappeared. Deva, one of our group from before I left town, came out of one of the back room doors. And when she didn't look the least bit surprised about the needles knitting on their own, I released a slow breath. So Deva was magical or whatever, too.

Was everyone in this town magical?

"So good to have you home. To stay this time, I hope. Sorry I'm late." She walked over to give the tabby cat a scratch under the chin. I hadn't even noticed him come back in. He and Marble were both curled up on different perches on the cat trees along the back wall.

"Lovely, Deva, thanks," he said, rubbing against her hand.

"Late?" I asked, confused.

Deva nodded.

"For what?"

"To initiate you into our world," she answered with a grin.

Oh boy.

Deva looked at the cat, then at me, then back at the cat. "I don't know what you know yet, except that because he talked in front of you, you obviously know he can."

I nodded mutely. Deva walked over and pulled one of the remaining arm chairs to be part of the cluster around Beth's desk before she plopped down on it beside me. "You all right?" she asked as she looked me over, her eyes lingering on my shoulder.

All I could seem to do was nod. I swallowed and sucked in a deep breath. "Yeah, apparently I'm Karma."

Deva sat back and gave me an appraising look. "Very cool. I've heard of that."

I looked between her and Carol and even glanced over at Beth, who was trying to wrap up her phone conversation. "This is just normal for you guys?"

Deva chuckled. "You poor thing." She leaned out of her chair so she could put one arm around me. "Yes, we've known we were witches for...Well, ever. Sounds like you've turned into one. It happens occasionally." She looked surprised for a second. "Hey, are you going home soon? I've got a big bag of food in my car for your brother and his girl-friend. You wanna take it with you?"

"Sure," I said, then swallowed hard around the lump in

my throat. Deva always had this way of tearing down my walls and making it hard to hide my emotions. And the fact that my old friends had obviously been helping a lot with my brother since I was gone made me feel like I wanted to cry and thank them, all at the same time.

"Things haven't been easy for you since you left," she said, her voice gentle as she watched me too closely.

I nodded, blinking back tears.

"I'm here for you. Always." Her dark eyes seemed to stare right into my soul.

I stood from my chair and held out my arms, waiting. Deva knew what I was asking for without me having to explain it and she pushed up from her chair so I could pull her into a tight hug. I squeezed her until she grunted.

"Thank you," I whispered, before turning and looking at Carol over my shoulder. "And thank you, too. For taking care of them."

Once I released Deva, I sat back down and looked around the room, not sure how to process everything.

"Want to talk about the whole magic thing first? Or what you've been up to?" Deva asked.

Magic thing. This was real. I wasn't human anymore. Which meant I could do things. But what? What were the limitations of magic? Did it even have any? So far I'd seen people reduced to toads, tires explode, people vanish, yarn knitting itself, and, of course, the talking cats. What if this was just the tip of the iceberg? Could people raise the dead? What about teleportation, was that real? All kinds of questions flooded my mind.

"Magic," I mumbled, pressing a hand to my forehead. Was I feeling light-headed or was this magic place actually swaying under my feet?

Deva grabbed her purse. "Here," she said and reached

inside. "Eat this." She produced a large chocolate bar, one of the good brands from overseas. "It'll help."

I nodded, because hell, why wouldn't chocolate help at this point? I certainly thought it would help when my ex had filed for divorce and when I found out he was boning his secretary. The wrapper crinkled as I opened it, the paper and foil tearing to reveal the creamy milk chocolate hidden underneath. I took a bite and immediately felt calmer. Like it was going to be okay. Like *everything* was going to be okay. Not just the magic stuff, but my divorce, the business, Henry and Alice. Everything would work out.

"Come on, dove," Deva said as she stood and pulled her purse over her shoulder before extending a hand to me. "Let me drive you home."

"I'll follow in her car," Carol offered. "Beth, we'll catch you up later!"

I took Deva's hand and she towed me from the chairs toward the door. Glancing over my shoulder, I saw that Beth was still on the phone. She waved, but I was too calm and happy to really process it. Why wouldn't I be happy? I had magical powers. That was enough to make anyone happy. Even the chime above Beth's door sounded happy as we went out.

After I vaguely pointed out my vehicle to Carol, I handed her my keys. Why wouldn't I trust her to get my car home with me? If she wanted to drive then so be it. Deva tugged on my hand again and we walked arm in arm around to the back of the little strip mall where her car was parked. It was a sleek black sedan that seemed to glow under the lights on the back of the building.

Deva got me strapped into her passenger seat, then she ran around to the drivers side, sliding in and throwing the car into reverse before she'd even finished buckling her seatbelt. She looked at me and grinned before we took off. "My chocolate should be working really well by now."

"Your chocolate?" I asked, feeling my brows furrowed in confusion. Was that something I'd ever noticed before? Being able to feel the muscles on my face moving with my expressions?

"Yeah, I wrapped it in one of those wrappers of the brand they sell at the airport. But I made it. My food makes people feel certain ways. I can do a lot with my food, good and bad." Deva's voice kept me from focusing too much on the strange sensation in my face.

I nodded, understanding. I mean, why wouldn't she be able to use food to make people feel things if Carol could knit without touching the needles and Beth could talk to animals? Was it the chocolate that was making my face feel funny?

"You'll remember all this tomorrow, but it'll be an easier pill to swallow after a good dose of that chocolate. Have another bite."

I did as she asked, even though I hadn't remembered the chocolate bar was still in my hands, and another wave of contentment washed over me. I licked the gooey bits from my fingers where I'd been holding it, enjoying the feel of the silky substance on my tongue.

"This is going to be great," I muttered.

"That's the spirit!" Deva laughed as though she knew a secret I didn't. She pulled her car up to a house that I assumed belonged to my brother's girlfriend. A woman came out the front door and stood on the porch, fiddling with the cuffs of her cardigan. "Come on, have you met her yet?"

I shook my head. Technically I had, but she'd been young then. I didn't know her as an adult, or as my brother's girlfriend.

I got out as Deva did the same, grabbing the bag of food from the backseat. As we walked up to the porch, I realized it wasn't just her fiddling with her clothing that let me know how painfully shy she was, but the way she couldn't hold my gaze. The way her eyes darted around, checking on every-thing as though she was worried something was out of place. Everything about her said that she was uncomfort-able around people.

I wondered why.

Under the oatmeal-colored cardigan she wore a pale pink chambray shirt that was unbuttoned just at the collar and some jeans with a pair of fuzzy bunny slippers, the kind where the ears moved as she walked. Her hair was pulled back in a tight bun, the auburn locks straining for their free-dom. From the looks of things, she had natural curls or at least waves in her hair that made it bunch up in sections even though she'd tried to pull it as tight as she could. Dark, doe eyes watched us from under a thick layer of lashes. She had a natural, no-makeup-required beauty that made most women probably want to scream. I was just glad that my brother had found someone who seemed just as quirky as he was.

Alice smiled and ducked her eyes. "I'm so happy to meet you," she said in a soft voice after Deva introduced us. "Your brother has told me so much about you."

She was just perfect, and that wasn't the chocolate talk-ing. Maybe a little off, considering she was mid-thirties and still wearing bunny slippers and having people watch out for her, but so was my brother. Together it seemed like they would be spot on.

There was no staying to chat, no inviting us in. It was a quick introduction, then Alice scurried back inside with her food and we got in the car and drove up the road to my place. Or maybe I should say Henry's place, since I hadn't lived there in so long. Our place. All I knew was that it wasn't my parent's house anymore.

Deva's voice broke through my inner ramblings as she said, "Alice is a witch, but her magic is a little off. Every time she tries a spell or potion it backfires, sometimes in hilarious ways, but also problematic ways. We keep an eye on her."

"I missed this. People keeping an eye on each other. My old neighbors would call the cops if my grass got too long," I said with a snort.

"If they call the cops here, at least it would be one of the cute, young officers that came out to see you." Deva chuckled.

Bring on the eye candy. After being married to Rick for years, I needed some. Despite myself, I thought of Daniel. It was stupid. He was just some guy I'd run into in a store and made a fool of myself in front of, but his bright green eyes seemed to float through my thoughts, and the memory of his smile made something inside of me ache. Like a yearning I couldn't explain. And just the feel of that yearning made me think of Rick cheating on me all over again.

I didn't want that jerk to still be hurting me, but somehow he was. Somehow even the thought of a handsome man's smile made me think of pain instead of love and potential. Had my ex broken something inside me? And could it be fixed?

The chocolate was good, but that could only get me so

far, unless Deva had some other chocolate to help with a broken heart.

I'd have to ask her about that.

7

EMMA

Carol was rocking in one of the old, weathered rocking chairs on the front porch when we got there, with my car parked in the spot on the left, the one that opened out onto the walkway to the front door. Deva eased into the driveway beside my car, and my gaze was fixed to Carol. For some reason, time seemed to slip away, and I remembered her waiting for me after school on the front porch when I had track practice. She would have the same far away look on her face back then. Only she was thinking about Bryan. They'd been sweethearts, the kind everyone thought would get married, until he'd had to move junior year.

She'd sworn that he was the one, and that she would wait as long as it took to get him back. But I couldn't imagine, even after all these years, that she was still thinking of him in these moments. She had to have moved on. Right?

I'd have to ask her about it. Because the only thing I could think of that would be worse than having your heart broken by a cheating ex was losing someone who could've really been it, and then spending your life missing them.

"Come on, let's go inside," Deva said, flashing her teeth in a quick grin.

I nodded, feeling strange. Happy but caught in my own thoughts too. Deva was beside my door a second later and pulled it open for me. Somehow, I remembered to unbuckle my seatbelt, and then we headed for the porch. My mind felt like candy floss, like it had been whipped around until it was as light as air and barely there at all. It wasn't unpleasant at all, but maybe a little disorienting.

The look vanished from Carol's face, and she smiled as she saw us heading toward her. "Feeling good?" she asked, tossing me my keys.

I couldn't help but return her smile and nodded as I unlocked the front door and threw my keys on the table inside the door. Then froze. The happy, relaxed feeling faded away and a cold shiver moved down my spine. I lifted my arm and stared down at it, realizing that every hair was standing on end. It was more than just goosebumps. This was every hair follicle pushing, every atom of my being telling me something had changed. Then I dropped my arm.

Before I even stepped forward to let Carol and Deva in, I knew deep in my soul that something was very, very wrong.

It felt like the floor was tilted under my feet as I let my gaze roam over the room. There was blood on the floor. Not a lot of it, but a small pool. And there were splatters around it.

If Henry was injured, it would be a bad injury, but he'd be okay. It didn't explain why he hadn't called me or why he was nowhere to be seen. I moved forward, taking in the rest of the living room as my eyes darted away from the pool of blood. It was trashed. Furniture had been tossed around. Vases and lamps that my parents had bought were shattered on the ground. And yet, the TV was tossed on its side, not stolen. Nothing seemed to be taken. So if this wasn't a robbery, what was it?

"Henry!" My feet crunched on glass as I began to move, looking to the bright windows that faced the sea. The white sand was still perfect, no tracks, no scuffle marks, nothing. The waves still rolled in and out as if my brother hadn't been hurt. But there was no sign of him. "Henry!" I shouted again, panic uncurling in my belly.

Behind me, I could sense my friends were standing in shocked silence. I told myself that I should keep going through the house. Maybe he was somewhere inside? And yet, my instinct said otherwise.

"Deva, could you call the police?" My words came out hollow.

It was the thing to do. Right? In situations like this, people called the police?

My heartbeat filled my ears, and Deva's voice was somewhere in the distance. I moved through the house like a nightmare, seeing more destruction with every step I took. Flashes of the car accident came into my mind, rising like a shadow around me until it was all my mind could focus on. My parents had been talking in the front seat. Henry had been asleep beside me. Headlights had seemed to fill the windshield, and I remembered the look of horror on my mom's face.

The memory moved in slow motion, just like I moved in slow motion through the house, fighting my mind to see what was in front of me and not what had happened in the past. I checked the bathroom and saw nothing to indicate Henry had cleaned and bandaged an injury, but saw toiletries thrown everywhere. The car appeared in my mind almost larger than life right at the moment when the glass shattered like an explosion. I remembered the front of the car crushing in, almost swallowing my parents, and then the car had teetered and started to roll over and over again.

Henry had called my name that night.

I called his name now, over and over again as I stared at his room, which was destroyed. Even his expensive computer monitors had been smashed in, and his sheets ripped and thrown about the room. Then I went to what was currently my room. I doubted he'd been in our parent's bedroom since they died. But still, I searched the room and my bathroom, praying he might have thought to hide in there, but I found the same destruction as the rest of the house, and no Henry.

That night came again, swallowing me as I stood in the center of a room filled with my destroyed belongings. The car had rolled until it was upside down. My back had felt like it'd been torn in half and blood was everywhere. But Henry was so scared beside me. So I'd unbuckled us both, which wasn't an easy feat given the strain our weight was putting on them as we hung there, and crawled through that broken glass.

I looked at my palm and saw the scars. I felt my knees twinge at the memory.

But I'd led Henry out of there. I'd climbed with him to the road, encouraging him every step of the way, where a stray passerby had seen us and called the police. My parents, there was nothing of them. Nothing that looked like the people I knew. Nothing that could indicate they were still alive.

I couldn't save them.

But I'd saved Henry.

And now? Now something was wrong. He wasn't here. Tears filled my vision, and I squeezed my hands closed, as if I could still feel the broken shards of glass that had been embedded beneath my skin. It was my job to protect him. I'd failed him so many times over the years. I'd let my friends take care of him instead of me. I should've told my ex that we had to move here. Not just cried and begged him to. I should've realized a man who didn't care about anything that was important to me wasn't the knight on a white horse I'd made him out to be. I'd thought he'd give me the life of my dreams, but all we had pursued were his dreams. Mine never mattered. But now that I was home, now that I was *here* for Henry, he was gone? Hurt?

"Where is he?" I sobbed, big, fat tears rolling down my cheeks as I scanned the room once more before I turned back to the living room and walked down the hall as my vision swam and I began to hiccup.

Someone had righted the kitchen table and chairs. Deva said nothing, just pulled me into one of them, and stared into my face. Maybe she was speaking. Saying something. I wasn't sure. I felt so far away. So lost.

Deva put her arm around me and hummed softly, her voice strangely soothing as time passed with no meaning, and then I heard the sound of sirens in the distance. Sounds and lights came sharply back to me, and I realized Deva was whispering, "It's okay. I'm here." Over and over again.

I turned toward her, and it was like everything was clicking back into place. My brother, the guy who never left the house, who didn't raise his voice, who wouldn't hurt a fly; He seemed to have been attacked. And our home was vandalized. Why? It made no sense.

Carol came back to us and sat down on a chair across from me. I didn't know what she'd been doing, but she was pale. Had she seen something I hadn't? Did she know something I didn't know?

"Who would do this?" I said, the words tearing from my lips.

Deva and Carol exchanged a look that made my stomach do a flip. Deva's dark brows drew together and then she spoke softly. "Before the police get here, Emma, listen. Your brother—the crew he was hanging with was pretty dangerous."

"Crew?" I stared at her in confusion. My brother didn't have a *crew*.

"He never mentioned anything?"

I shook my head, shocked. The fact that he had a girlfriend had astounded me considering I knew he hated leaving the house, but now to learn he had a whole crew of friends? How much had my brother changed while I'd been gone? "I thought he mostly just hung around with Alice and stayed here," I murmured, almost more to myself than anyone else.

They exchanged another knowing glance, and I pulled away from Deva. They knew something. That much was clear. My shoulders were like stone, and my panic was fading, replaced by confusion.

"Tell me. Please. I need to understand."

Carol sighed and ran a hand through her light brown hair. "Henry can count cards."

I stared at her dumbly. I hadn't known that, but it made sense. He was that smart. "Okay?"

What did that have to do with any of this? He always liked to collect action figures and rare collectibles of nerdy things that he loved. And I was pretty sure he dominated everyone in games online.

Deva squeezed my shoulders. "He got into gambling, and then he got into gambling with the vampires."

Gambling with vampires? Is that what she just said? My

brother, my sweet brother, was gambling with bloodsucking animals that burned in the light and wore capes? I couldn't believe it. Talking cats, fine. Karma powers, okay. Gambling vampires? No. Just no.

"W-hat?" I stuttered out.

"He's really good," Carol said, as if that would make any of this make sense. "But from the rumors, he always takes it a step too far and loses."

And it was like everything clicked in my mind.

"That's why he was always asking for money," I whispered, a rush of cold air moving over my skin as things that never made sense suddenly did.

Deva reached out and squeezed my good shoulder. "Yeah, he asked for it from all of us once or twice. But the thing is, you can't tell the sheriff."

"Why not?" I cried. "If the vampires have him, we have to get him back." I would pay his debt, even if it cost me every last penny.

"There are others that can help us with that," Carol said. "Not the human police." She looked at Deva again. "Honestly, we probably shouldn't have called them."

The more I was learning about this supernatural world, the more I was starting to hate it.

Suddenly, someone knocked loudly on the door, and my gut tensed. My head was spinning from everything I'd seen and heard, but one thing pushed in front of the rest. If I started blabbing about vampires and gambling, I wasn't going to get helped by humans, I was going to get locked up. That much I knew.

So, I let them in and explained what happened, keeping it vague. They took a bunch of pictures and asked questions about Henry and who he hung around with, but I was able to honestly answer that I didn't know. I didn't know his friends outside of Alice.

Behind the officers, I sensed someone else come in. My heart leapt as for a split second I thought it had to be Henry. I stepped away from them, my gaze searching for my brother, and froze as Daniel's big form seemed to fill the doorway. For some reason, just the sight of the big man with his kind green eyes made me want to run to him. He seemed like the kind of man who could take all your worries away and swallow you in a hug that made the world seem less frightening.

His eyes found mine, and it was like for one minute someone in this world not only saw how much I was hurting, he felt it too. My vision blurred as more tears filled my eyes, and he took a step forward, as if to offer me comfort.

Carol stepped in front of him. "Daniel, I'm glad you were working today."

The moment between us shattered, and he looked away from me, his gaze on her.

I felt like a deflated balloon. Daniel was a big man, with strong arms, and the kind of face that women dreamed of. But he wasn't mine. He was just a ghost from my past here to do his job.

"He only works part-time since his wife died," Deva whispered in my ear, and I realized I must have been staring. I could have told her that I knew that already, but I didn't want to deprive her of giving me the tidbits of gossip she thought I'd appreciate.

Daniel arched an eyebrow and glanced at Deva. Had he heard her? No, not from so far away. There must have been a different reason for that knowing look of his, one that said he knew exactly what Deva was briefing me on.

Carol put her hand on his arm. "I think this is a case you'll want to take a special interest in."

I tensed. What did that mean? I thought we weren't supposed to tell them anything? And why did Carol seem to be so close to him? The question bothered me in a way I didn't understand, or didn't want to understand at least.

But he simply nodded, glancing at me once more before he said, "Okay, boys, I'll take it from here. Henry is a family friend." He spoke to the officers as if he was their boss. And to my surprise, even without him actually being sheriff anymore, they all quickly obeyed him, clearing out of the room with barely a look in my direction.

The next thing I knew, we were all sitting at the kitchen table. All eyes were suddenly on me, as though I had any idea what had happened here. I needed answers, not questions. I needed action, not sitting still while under the watchful green eyes of Daniel Arthur.

8

EMMA

"Okay, Emma, tell him the truth," Carol said. "Anything you know."

My gaze moved to Daniel. He studied me, and beneath his gentle expression, I could see his thoughts were turning. It was strangely interesting. I got the feeling that he was a really good cop. Which was dumb, because I'd never seen him do anything that logically told me that.

"Tell him what? I don't know anything."

Carol lifted a brow. "You can be *honest* with him."

Now, I was really confused. Was that just something she was saying, but if I started talking about vampire gambling rings he'd think I was a moron? How much could I really say to Daniel before he thought we were all crazy? Did he have the authority to place us, or rather me, under a psychiatric hold?

I probably couldn't say much if I wanted to keep my freedom.

I looked at Daniel and then back at Carol, choosing my words with care, which made me speak slowly and probably sound a little odd. "Every once in a while, Henry would ask me for a large sum of money. Well, large in my eyes. Several hundred, usually. Sometimes close to a thousand. I figured he was just managing his money poorly."

Carol shook her head. "No, it wasn't that."

Clearly. Because clearly, I couldn't do a proper job taking care of my brother when I wasn't even around him. Apparently, I wasn't good at being a wife or a sister, and now my brother might be in trouble because of it.

Deva set a tray down on the table, startling me. I hadn't even noticed she was making tea. And where had the cookies come from? She poured the tea as she talked, the amber liquid rushing into the cream-colored china cups, which had apparently been boring enough for the attackers to leave them alone. "Rumor has it that Henry has been gambling with the vampires and sometimes he loses pretty big."

Vampires. Okay. Cool. She said it. Totally fine.

I wasn't going to freak out.

Nope.

I inhaled slowly through my nose and held my breath, releasing it between my slightly parted lips, and hoped that no one noticed that I was on the edge of losing my shit. Again.

Now what?

Carol nodded, then when I still didn't jump in, she added, "And when he loses, supposedly it's usually against the shifters."

Shifters. Okay. We were doing that now. Sparkly vampires and growly, exploding clothes shifters. None of this was weird. Not at all. And it wasn't weird we were telling a human all of this, and that he wasn't looking at us like we were nuts. I'd seen movies about shit like this. Someone seeing something that no one else could. Everyone thinking they were crazy. At least I had Deva and Carol to back me up.

"Is that about it?" he asked, his expression unexpectedly frustrated.

Seriously?

Was that it?

I don't know. Did we want to add mermaids or witches to the story? Everything seemed so comical in that moment that I almost started giggling. It was the kind of laughter that only happened when things were too serious, or too awkward, or too ridiculous. I had to swallow a few times to prevent the giggle that was lodged in my chest from spilling out.

Deva grabbed her cup. "Yeah, that's about all we know. Sorry we can't be more helpful."

Daniel sighed. "I'll take care of it." He got up and started walking away, his cup of tea untouched.

"Wait." I jumped up, and he froze and looked back at me. "What are you going to do? Can I help?"

"Just stay here and be safe." He gave me a small smile.

"No. He's my brother." My hands curled into fists again, and that giggle that had been lodged in my chest morphed into a tempest of anger and hurt. I wasn't sure if I was going to start screaming or crying.

He moved closer to me and ducked his head a little, so we were eye-to-eye. "I'm going to do everything I can to make sure your brother is okay. Alright? I promise."

For some reason, I believed him. "Well, I'm not going to just sit here and do nothing."

His mouth curled into another small smile. "No, of course you aren't. You're Emma, the girl who can sing loud enough to shake the entire gymnasium."

I stared at him in surprise, not knowing what to say.

He bobbed his head, almost like he was giving me a little bow. "I'll let you know anything I find out."

As he turned to go, my gaze was locked on him. It was strange to me that in my forty-something years, I'd never met a man like him before. It didn't matter that I'd known him in high school. Well, known might be too strong a word. I'd crushed on him, hard. If he was anything like me, then he was vastly different than his high school self. Sure, the core was still the same, but experiences change you. I could only imagine how losing his wife had changed him.

His height and his strength should make him intimidating to me. But instead, he was so damn reassuring that I both wanted him to stay and wanted to push him on his way to find out anything he could about Henry.

Most of the time I was sure that a man would say one thing and do another. With Daniel, I believed him. Which probably made me an idiot.

At the door, he looked back at me one last time, wearing the same look he had in the grocery store, and those green eyes of his felt like they were trying to tell me something, but I didn't understand, and then he was gone. I rubbed my face, finding more tears on my cheeks, and turned back and headed for the dining room.

I returned to the table where Deva was putting a cup of tea in front of my seat. "Drink," she said. "It'll calm your nerves."

I put the glass to my lips but paused. "You're not going to get me high like with the chocolate are you?"

She chuckled and pushed the small plate with cookies on it toward me until it was next to my cup and saucer. "No, but it will calm your nerves. You won't feel quite so spacey though. Also eat a couple cookies. They'll help your shoulder heal faster. Like a lot faster."

I nodded. Calm was fine, but no more chocolate-drunk. If my shoulder could feel better as well? I was all for that since I hated wearing that damned sling.

"Where is he going?" I asked as I sipped on my tea before chowing down on a couple cookies, trying to figure out this whole strange situation, and why they'd felt comfortable telling him things we couldn't tell the other cops.

"The clubs. The vampires won't be at their club until nightfall, but the shifters hang out at all hours at their place."

It was strange. I would never want to hang out at some-place with hissing vampires and growling shifters. I'd had the sense that Daniel was brave before, but it took someone with a lot of guts to go to a place like that.

And he was doing it for me. Okay, not for me, but for my brother.

Yet, as much as I appreciated what he was doing, it wasn't enough. I'd watched enough crime shows to know the next twenty-four hours were the most important. If I didn't find my brother by then. I didn't want to think about that.

"Do you know what club he's going to?" I asked. I'd told him I wouldn't sit around and do nothing. Just because he'd given me a sweet smile and looked at me with those stupidly gorgeous eyes of his didn't mean I was going to suddenly change my mind.

Deva and Carol exchanged yet another glance. "I do," Deva said guardedly. "It's not really a club, per se. More of a shifter hangout spot."

I held her gaze. "Can you take me there?"

"I don't know. It can be dangerous."

"Please," I pleaded around my mouthful of cookie.

She frowned, shaking her head. "It's not a place we should be going to."

I laughed darkly. "I'm Karma, remember? What could go wrong?"

Carol snorted. "Famous last words."

Deva looked unsure, but finally gave a curt nod. "Fine, but I'm calling the others. That way they know where to find us and so we'll have backup if we need it."

Carol nodded. "Good idea. I could use a break from the shop."

"And we're stopping at my restaurant first." Deva stood. "I need to pick up a few things."

I didn't know why, but this was the first time in my life that I got a feeling picking things up from a restaurant was going to end in some magical trouble. But then again, I'd never expected magical trouble before. I also had the feeling that tracking down the people who took my brother might send karma flying around, so I had no idea which of us would be more dangerous.

Or even if we would stand a chance against the shifters.

9

EMMA

After a pitstop at Deva's restaurant, which was full of delicious-looking food that practically had me drooling over the display case, she drove Carol and I to—well, the middle of nowhere. The woods led right up to a cliff face, which the road we were on ran directly along. And if I was remembering the shape of the coastline correctly, it also dropped right into the ocean, which was a terrifying thought in and of itself, never mind adding in shifters that could turn into god-knows-what on top of that, probably running around in the forest.

The paved road beneath us suddenly ended just ahead of us, giving way to a bumpy dirt road that continued into seemingly nothing. Deva slowed down before we left the pavement, but we were still instantly tossed around like bags of potatoes, and my back didn't like that one bit.

I groaned and shifted around in my seat, clenching my teeth as one wheel caught a pothole.

"Your back?" Carol asked from the seat behind Deva.

I looked back at her, where she sat with her knitting gear clicking away in front of her, and sighed. "It bugged me when I was younger, but now there's not enough Advil in the world to get it to calm the heck down sometimes."

"Tell me about it. My knees ache every time I have to take the stairs to the apartment."

"That's nothing," Deva said, both hands firmly on the wheel. "Did I tell you what my chiropractor said about my neck?"

Carol spoke up, in an amused voice. "It's the *worst neck he's ever seen*."

Deva gave her a dirty look through the rearview mirror. "Hey, you guys started this whole, *we're old and we know it thing*."

"I didn't say I was old!" I exclaimed. I wasn't some spring chicken, but I also wasn't the one lying on its side wheezing —*most* of the time.

I pushed the thought of the wheezing chicken aside as my back gave another pang. If this ride lasted much longer, I might very well end up crawling out of the car when we stopped, looking very similar to a dying chicken. And I liked to think I was above that.

"We're not on death's door or anything," I mumbled.

Deva raised a brow. "No, your back just gets sore from car rides."

I lifted a brow. Everyone held their breath. And then I grinned, and we all started laughing. If we couldn't joke around about our failing bodies with each other, well, we weren't that good of friends after all.

"Can you imagine what we'll be like when we're in our seventies?" Carol asked with a smile.

"I just hope I live that long," Deva muttered, her gaze focused on the bumpy road in front of us.

I frowned. "Do witches live shorter lives than humans?"

Deva glanced at me in surprise, then back at the road. "Actually, the opposite, but I swear my ex is aging me."

"Yeah? He being a jerk?"

She shook her head. "No, actually, the opposite. I can't exactly complain about it around Beth, since her cheating ex is such a jerk, but Harry has been going out of his way to try to win me back. He's sending flowers, writing poems. He even stops by the house on trash day and puts the bins out before I wake up." She sighs. "I asked him to do those things for years. I begged him to turn off the sports, or take a break from the guys for a date night, or put out the trash without me asking until one day I just stopped asking. For too long he enjoyed doing everything he wanted without the nagging. He acted like his life was just awesome because I didn't need anything, and he could do whatever he wanted. But I just fell out of love with him. Every time I was alone. Every time I took the trash out by myself. Every time a birthday or holiday would pass without a gift..."

I smiled, but it was a sad smile. Most people could never understand what it felt like to be alone with someone else, but I did. "I understand."

"Do you?" she asked. "Because his family and my family are acting like I should just forgive him. That he understands what he did was wrong, and he's trying. The thing is, I didn't suddenly stop loving him when I asked for the divorce. I hadn't loved him in so long, and I'm honestly happier without him. I keep asking him to stop trying to win me back, but he, and our families, seem to think with enough time and effort I'll cave."

"You didn't need to say anything more than that you're happier without him. You don't need to justify yourself. Not to me, and not to anyone else."

She took one hand off the steering wheel and squeezed

mine for a second before returning it. "I forgot how much I missed you. Seriously. The phone calls were nice, but it wasn't like this."

"I know. I'm sorry," I said, and I meant it.

Deva was always so strong, even on the phone. She talked about her divorce like it was no big deal. And even before that, I knew Harry frustrated her at times, but I had no idea she was as lonely as I was. It seemed like such a terrible thing that we'd been suffering alone when we could've had each other.

"Did you tell her about Marquis?" Carol called from the back.

To my shock, Deva's cheeks turned a little red. "There's nothing to tell."

I looked back at Carol, and there was a glow to her face.

"What?" I asked, looking between them.

"We're here," Deva said, not-so-smoothly changing the subject.

"We're coming back to that later," I said, shaking my finger at her.

Carol gave that awesome loud laugh of hers that always warmed my heart. That's right. They knew I was damned stubborn. If there was some new guy in Deva's life, I wanted to hear all about it.

The rough path suddenly opened out into a clearing scattered with cars, chaos, and guys in every direction. My jaw dropped open as my gaze ran over everything, then landed on the buildings. Small cottages with thatched roofs were spread out around what looked like one larger central building. It could have been a cute little area, very homey.

Could being the operative word there.

"Where are we?" I whispered.

And was this how shifters lived?

Deva put her finger to her lips and looked around as she tapped her ears, reminding me that these shifters had excellent hearing and I shouldn't say anything negative about our surroundings. The reminder was a good one though. The last thing I wanted was to piss off a bunch of shifters.

Except that the place looked more than a little run down. Paint, on what was probably cedar siding on the houses, was peeling or gone completely. The thatches on the roof of each cottage looked like they were about to leap from their perch to their deaths by choice just to get away from the rundown state of the cottages. One was even missing a front door. A bead curtain that looked like it was from the seventies hung there instead, like this was some sort of hippie commune, except hippies would have taken better care of their things.

My gaze traveled over the smaller buildings, eventually landing on the larger one that sat in the middle. It looked like it could have been a meeting house of some kind with all the windows, or what would be windows if they weren't broken and boarded over. The place was long and could have fit a good-sized cafeteria inside. On the side closest to us, I noticed a large stone chimney that had been built. With the way the mortar was missing from between the large, naturally-shaped rocks, though? I wouldn't go anywhere near that thing.

In the central clearing between the cottages and the meeting house, there was a large fire pit and multiple charcoal grills around, along with lawn chairs that had clearly seen better days. My guess would be that they were left out come rain or shine and mother nature had taken her toll on them. There was also a trash barrel, one of the huge fifty-gallon ones, sitting over by a tree that was overflowing with beer cans and amber bottles of various shapes and sizes.

And when I say overflowing, I mean there were piles on the ground next to it, along with what could almost be described as a carpet of cans leading up to it.

Someone had either thrown a massive party and not cleaned up yet, or, my better guess, was that there were raucous parties every night and no one ever cleaned up. At least that was my hope, since it would explain the disrepair of the houses as well.

As I looked past the trashcan tree, I realized that it looked like they'd been playing paintball all over as well, with the trees serving as their targets, or maybe they were just all shitty shots and the trees caught all the badly aimed paintballs. When Deva killed the engine of the car, music blared in my ears, only getting louder as we stepped out of the car.

Ugh.

When we got out I noticed that my shoulder didn't hurt, like, at all, which was crazy. I paused and slipped the sling over my head, stretching my arm out, which felt amazing. I caught Deva watching and smiled before pointing to my shoulder and giving her a thumbs up. I had no idea what she did to those cookies, but if they could fix my shoulder that well then maybe I could get a constant supply for my back as well?

As we walked around the various trucks and cars that were parked haphazardly and moved closer to the group of men hanging out, I noticed that Deva had a box in her hand with her restaurant logo on it.

I froze when one of them took a running start and jumped off the cliff. He screamed as he fell, then his yells cut off with a distant splash. Without waiting nearly long enough for the first jumper to swim out of the way, another one sprinted toward the edge of the cliff, launching himself in the air and posing for a split second before falling out of my line of sight. Honestly, this place felt more like a frat house than anything else. It almost smelled like one as well, the faint tang of stale beer and blood on the breeze, along with old, sweaty socks.

Where were the parents? Where were the responsible adults? Did shifters even have any?

Suddenly, I wished I'd asked Deva more about them. Heck, I wished I'd asked her more questions in general. With everything that had happened with my ex, I'd been feeling low in general. But with my brother going missing, it felt like the cloud that had shadowed me for weeks was suddenly all around me. And if I didn't fight through it, I was just going to handle this search for my brother in a daze.

I couldn't do that. I needed to do better and keep my wits about me.

Silently, I promised myself I would.

The three of us moved forward with most of the guys ignoring us. Standing off to the side, I glanced at Deva then at Carol, waiting to see what the protocol was for something like this, or for anyone to acknowledge our presence.

Eventually, I got tired of waiting. I'm not the most patient person at the best of times, and this was most definitely not the best of times. "Hello?" I called. "Could I please speak to the person in charge?"

One young man stood up from a lawn chair, large, imposing, and mean-looking. His hair was dark and left a little long, and he had a scruff of beard on his almost-attractive face. He seemed to be maybe in his early twenties, but his massive build made him appear deceptively older. There was also something unsettling about the way his pale gray eyes seemed to narrow in on me before a snarl twisted his lips and he began walking toward us.

My stomach flipped, and I tried to remind myself my son was probably nearly the same age. I still saw twenty-something-year-olds as children. And yet, I'd never been unsettled and a little frightened by a child before.

I reminded myself it was probably because he was a shifter, even if he didn't appear to have long claws and fur sprouting from every inch of him. My gaze slid around to the other young men. Some of them drank, eyes glazed over. A couple tossed a ball back and forth, but there was no heart in the game. And many studied us, but with an almost complete lack of interest. I looked back at the man heading toward me. What was this place? Some kind of Neverland where kids grew to become young men without any goals or guidance?

"The alpha died. This is his son and the new alpha," Deva whispered, as if reading my thoughts.

"That's right," he said in a growly voice, even though he should've been too far away to hear her quiet words. "So show some respect." He bared his teeth like a dog about to attack.

Show him some respect, because he inherited a position? Unlikely. I arched one eyebrow. Sure, he was big and scary, but he was also like twenty. He should've been showing *me* some respect. He had nothing on me when it came to life experience. Hell, most of these guys were still dressed like they were in college or high school. All hoodies, baseball caps, and torn jeans.

Evidently raising an eyebrow wasn't showing respect, though. He noticed my facial expression and snapped one finger. The rest of the guys, mostly his age or younger, jumped to their feet and the next thing I knew, we were surrounded, with the boys—totally not men, *boys*—slowly closing the circle.

Fear bloomed in my gut. Damn my resting bitch face! It wasn't bad enough that even when I wasn't particularly upset I looked pissed but why did my every single damn emotion have to show on my face? I could never play poker.

The thought reminded me why we were there in the first place. Henry. The group he'd sicced after us moved ever closer, and the alpha's expression was purely murderous, even though he was still standing well back.

Oh man, we'd made a huge mistake coming here.

If Deva or Carol got hurt because of me and my bull-headedness or my resting bitch face, I'd never forgive myself. They had only just come back into my life. I wasn't ready for them to be gone, or for me to bite it at the jaws of some punkass shifter kids. I could feel my heart galloping in my chest as though it was trying to break through my ribs and take the shifters on itself, or run away. Actually, probably the latter. It was the urge to turn and run that I was having trouble ignoring at that moment. But if running from a shifter was anything like running from a wild animal, especially a wolf or something like that, then my actions would only increase the danger we were in. It was that fact that kept my feet firmly planted where they were.

"Enough of this," Deva snapped as she stepped forward. "Have you lost your damn mind?"

The alpha stopped and I realized that he'd been emitting a low growl the entire time. It was only as he stopped and stared at Deva in shock that I noticed the lack of it. When he hesitated, so did the rest of his pack.

Deva wasn't done. "You stop this right now." She strode forward, shouldering her way through the circle of shifters that had been advancing on us, and put her finger right in his face, and the enormous, towering man-child actually shrank back. "Your father would be ashamed of you, Nathan. Absolutely mortified. He never ran his pack like this. It's not a party."

She turned and looked at each of them, stacking her hands on her hips. No one escaped her glare. If she was my mom, her flip-flop would have been off and in her hand as an unspoken threat, but that may have been taking it a little too far with these shifters. "What do you have to say for yourselves?"

If I hadn't been standing here watching it happen, I wouldn't have believed it. I glanced at Carol just to make sure we were seeing the same thing, and she had a knowing smile on her face. They took off their hats, dropped their heads, displaying their epic hat hair, and from what I could tell, each of them mumbled apologies.

"Now," Deva continued. "Get this bullshit cleaned up before I go find all of yall's mamas. I can't believe how badly you're disrespecting nature. Get that paint off the trees. You think mother nature will put up with your shit forever? Don't make her have to tan your hides."

All of the pack stood frozen until Deva pointed at two of them and snapped her fingers. "You two, clean the paint off the trees." She pointed at two more. "You two, get all the trash up and in bags. Now. And make sure to sort out the recycling."

Everyone ran into action, except for the alpha, Nathan. He stood as if waiting for further direction. "Go help," Deva said, sounding exasperated. "You're not above cleaning up your mess!"

The three of us moved to one side and sat on their yard chairs as we watched while they scurried around the clearing. The guys who had jumped off the cliff came up and saw all the hullabaloo, then immediately ducked their heads and got busy. It didn't matter that they were dripping wet, they just joined in and started cleaning.

When it looked quite a bit better, Deva sat up. "Nathan," she called. "We have a question for you."

He walked up, pulling his ball cap off once more and flexing his hand around the bill, curving it even more, looking all contrite. "Yes?"

One arched eyebrow from Deva was all it took. She was going to have to give me lessons. Apparently my arched eyebrow pissed people off while hers commanded respect. I must have been doing something wrong. He blinked rapidly. "Yes, ma'am?"

"Emma here has a question for you."

The young alpha turned to face me, since I was sitting slightly off to the side from where Deva was. His gray eyes looked stormy, but the way his eyebrows pinched together told me that he truly regretted his earlier actions, or at least regretted being called on them.

"I'm looking for my brother," I said. "Henry Foxx."

His eyes widened dramatically, the gray circles of his irises perfectly visible. "Henry?" He dragged the hand not holding his ball cap over his mouth and the stubble that sporadically decorated his face. His eyes were full of apology as he said, "Man, that dude is in *big* trouble."

10

EMMA

"What are you talking about? What trouble?" I demanded as Nathan stumbled back slightly at the tone of my voice. He couldn't talk fast enough to calm my racing heart.

This side of Henry was completely new to me. Getting in trouble? Gambling? Gambling with shifters and vamps? Lying to me? My brother had changed so much. Part of me wondered if Alice knew what he was up to and that was why they still hadn't moved in together. Or maybe they were just that quirky.

Nathan shifted on his feet, switching his weight from one side to the other and back again, as though he was physically uncomfortable with the conversation. "People thought Henry was counting cards. The other night he won a ton of money. Before he could leave, the whole club turned on him, shifters and vampires alike. Asking how he was winning so much and so on."

"What happened?" I cried, bolting upright from where I'd been sitting on the edge of the lawn chair. "Where is he?"

"He tried to explain with a bunch of math jargon, but it

was confusing and high-level. It only pissed everyone off worse. He would have been better off keeping his mouth shut." Nathan shrugged.

I wasn't sure I believed that he shouldn't have said anything. If it was me and someone stayed silent in the face of accusations, I'd take that as an admission of guilt. I could understand why it only pissed them off even more when Henry started talking math at them. My brother wasn't exactly easy to understand when it came to that subject. His knowledge was just so in-depth and, if I was honest, over-whelming that I can understand them getting pissed off.

"Tell me where he is," I demanded as I took a step toward the alpha, the fear leaving my voice and being replaced by anger.

"They'd gathered he was doing something like counting cards. Even convinced the owner of the club that he was. After he won big, he got a lot of threats, but the Vampire Mistress that runs the vampires wouldn't let them hurt Henry. I think because he's human, or maybe she has a soft spot for him. I don't really know. Either way, she warned him about not coming back unless he wanted trouble. And we all know what vamps mean when they say trouble."

"Then what? He's not home, and there's been an inci-dent at the house. Would any of your shifters have gone after him even after the Vampire Mistress said not to?"

Nathan shook his head, swiping the air with his hand to emphasize his point. "We've all been here, goofing off and recovering after a big party last night. I'd be surprised if one of my guys went against the Vampire Mistress. But I wouldn't put much past those vampires. There's some polit-ical bullshit mixed up in there that might make them want to do the opposite of what she ordered."

Great. Political bullshit with the vampires had just been

added to the list of things I needed to figure out about the supernatural world.

They should really make a handbook or something. *So You've Become Karma*. Or *The Supernatural: The Real, the Fake, the Weird*. I'd totally read both of those. It would be like the *Handbook for the Recently Deceased* but, you know, for the supernatural.

Deva stood and looked around. I followed her gaze and was surprised to find how much they'd accomplished while we'd been talking. The trees were clean of the paint splatters that had been covering them when we arrived, but the bark was still in place, which was good. I had been worried when Deva asked them to clean it that they'd choose a more destructive path to accomplish the goal.

All the beer cans, bottles, and general trash that had been around the area had been picked up and bagged. The overflowing trash can had even been emptied. I wasn't surprised when I noticed a stack of trash bags by the meeting house, but I was surprised to see a number of green bags as well. They'd followed their orders and separated out the recycling. They could be taught!

We couldn't do much to fix up the actual cottages, but the area had been vastly improved already. Even the grills around the fire pit had been cleaned, the silver bars shining in the light, and pushed back toward the cottages that I assumed they came from. The fire pit itself had been restocked with wood and a fire was just starting to glow within the stack of logs that had been placed within it. They had even moved extra over to the side where the grills had been sitting.

I would actually spend time here now. Maybe not stay in one of the cottages, but I'd come out for a bonfire or a cookout. When I looked over at Deva, she was smiling. It was a small, satisfied smile, but it was there nonetheless.

She took a deep breath and as she held out the box I'd seen her carrying earlier, she said, "Thank you, boys. Please don't treat nature like this anymore. You're better than this. Your father would have wanted better than this for the pack. Respect what our world has given you, understand?"

They all sort of lined up and nodded at her, contrite. There were a lot of muttered, "Yes, ma'am's" through the crowd, even from Nathan himself.

One guy, however, sighed softly under his breath and mumbled, "Old ladies always want everything cleaned." Then he turned, heading toward the cliff.

I glared. Who was he to call us old? And then he tripped, epically, his hands flailing out around him before hitting the ground. Everyone turned to look at him. The guys started laughing. He turned and frowned down, as if searching for what could've tripped him. Except, there was nothing on the ground.

I felt Deva and Carol staring at me.

My cheeks felt hot as I looked at them. *Oops.* I really had to learn how to control this whole karma thing before someone figured out what I could do.

"Well, uh, thanks again for the info," I said, giving an awkward wave.

Nathan was grinning at the guy on the ground. "No worries." Then he shouted toward him, "Fall came a little early this year, huh?"

I rolled my eyes. Man, I did *not* miss being twenty sometimes. I liked to think I had never been so obnoxious, but the truth was I probably was.

We turned and began to walk back to Deva's car. It wasn't far, but we did have to weave through the trucks and cars once again. As we left I heard Nathan say, "Hell yeah, donuts!" I guess that answered the question of what was in the box.

"Are shifters normally clumsy?" I asked softly.

Deva snorted. "No. The opposite. That was all you."

Darn. I was kind of hoping I was wrong, but I guess I should be growing accustomed to all these weird things being connected to me. I just wondered if I should feel bad about it or just accept that my powers knew what they were doing.

"That's what he gets for calling us old," Carol whispered.

I grinned. Okay, so this one I wouldn't feel guilty about. "Glad my uncontrollable powers are funny to you."

"Oh, they are," Deva said, a twinkle in her eyes. "But you should've seen us when we were learning to use our powers. It was, well, it was a mess."

I thought of them in high school and frowned, my thoughts combing over a thousand tiny moments. But I couldn't think of a single moment that suggested they were somehow trying to balance being teens and being witches. I was going to have to ask them about it one day.

Just as we reached the sedan, a truck pulled up next to our car. An old blue pickup with peeling paint. And who should be in the truck? No one other than Daniel himself.

I hated that my pulse sped up a little. His arm was lying along his open window, and the breeze had ruffled his auburn hair. His tanned skin was a little flush, and his gaze locked with mine, his expression unreadable. He seemed so wild in that moment, almost like this was how he was meant to be, that my breath caught a little. My ex was never the kind of guy who left the windows down, even though I loved the feeling of the breeze on my face. Did Daniel feel free in the wind the way I did?

"Hey," he called. "What are you doing here?"

I debated about not telling him, but the impulse was dumb. He knew why we were there. I just hoped that he didn't think we didn't trust him. Yeah, most of the reason I trusted him was some stupid instinct that said I could, but the feeling was still there. And it wasn't something I could ignore. Nor could I pretend the idea of hurting him didn't bother me.

"We had to look into it," I said. "I'm sorry."

I knew he'd said he would talk to them, but he wasn't moving fast enough for me. Then again, most people didn't. Something about burning the candle at both ends for years as I built my business had created this strange person inside of me that had to do everything myself, and right away. Some small part of me knew it was because if I waited on my ex to do anything, it wouldn't get done. But this situation wasn't just about my control issues, as toad-man had called them, it was about getting my brother home safely, at all costs.

Daniel smiled after a moment, and my gaze pulled to his soft-looking lips. "A guy stops for a few minutes to check out some police reports, and ends up running behind. I guess I should've expected that from Emma and the Private Psych crew."

"Private Psych crew?" I asked, frowning.

He glanced toward Carol and Deva. "Didn't they tell you that little shop of Beth's is more than just catching cheaters? These ladies end up being involved in a lot of supernatural investigations, and they end up solving a lot of them too."

I glanced at my friends. "Really? You guys acted like it was no big deal."

Carol shrugged, a grin stretching her lips. "You know I'm not one to brag."

Man, I was impressed. My friends really had done a lot since I was gone.

"For the record," he said, drawing me from my thoughts. "I don't think the shifters are involved, but we still need to talk." He glanced over at where Nathan and the boys were still semi lined up, confused looks on their faces, and I could see the questions dancing in his eyes as he looked back at us.

Carol got a guilty look and headed for the car, as did Deva. So I followed them, wondering how typical it was for Deva to be able to command a bunch of unruly people to obey her.

"I agree. They don't seem to know anything, but someone does," I said as I slid into the passenger seat of Deva's car. I automatically reached for the seatbelt with what should be my bum arm, but just as I'd thought when I got out of the car, it didn't hurt any more. I silently rejoiced at having full functionality of both my arms once more.

"I'm not going to be able to stop you from looking into this, am I?" Daniel's voice sounded amused and exasperated at the same time.

I shook my head.

He was staring at me in a strange way. "You haven't changed one bit."

"How do you know?" I asked, truly curious.

He finally looked away. "I'm a shifter. I notice more than you think."

I stiffened. Daniel was a shifter? So many things that hadn't made sense clicked into place. "So shifters notice specific things about everyone?"

"Not everyone," he said softly, then turned off his engine and started to climb out. "You ladies be careful out there. Not that you will."

"I'll do whatever I have to in order to get my brother back." The words left my mouth before I could think, but I didn't regret them. I meant them with every fiber of my being.

He shook his head and headed toward the guys.

No doubt he thought I was crazy. He may as well learn that I did my own thing, or at least that's who I was remembering to be, who I was before Rick. Before I was manipulated into being someone I wasn't. Before I had to turn my personality down so I didn't overshadow my husband. The toad.

A vindictive part of me hoped he stayed like that forever.

I pushed the thought aside as I pictured Daniel sprouting hair and roaring at the moon. Or was it howling? Right now, I cared a little less about the old toad than the shifter thing.

My heart hammered as I closed my door. "I have a lot of questions."

"About shifters or Daniel?" Deva asked, a smile in her voice.

Daniel glanced back toward us.

Darn it. Had he heard her? "About shifters, of course."

Deva turned on the engine and pulled away. "Shoot."

But before I started in on a subject I was sure was going to be complicated, I couldn't help but ask, "Could we drive with the windows down?"

Deva nodded and smiled. "You always did love the windows down."

"But somehow I forgot," I said softly. "I forgot a lot about who I was and what I liked."

"You're remembering though. And soon you'll not just remember who you were, but you'll find out who you are now. It takes some time, but you will. It was like that with me for a while after my divorce." Deva didn't wait for a response, she just unrolled the windows.

Cool, crisp autumn air rushed in around us, and I closed my eyes. So much had changed, but I was happy to know not everything had. I still felt free like this. And maybe for the first time in a long time, it wasn't just the wind that made me feel free; it was the sense that I was finding the life I was always meant to find. Of that I was certain.

I didn't even care that it'd taken me forty-two years. I was just glad I wasn't wasting anymore time being unhappy. Because no one was guaranteed a tomorrow.

Even with the bumpy road, that was the best drive I'd had in years.

11

DANIEL

I'd always thought she was human.

As Emma, Carol, and Deva drove away, I shook my head. The woman was fascinating, and I would've laid down money she'd never known about this world before. What had changed in her life to give her the knowledge or some power of her own? And for that matter, what was she? What kind of powers did she have now? Or was she truly just a human in the know?

When she was human, or when I'd thought she was human, she'd been off limits. Did that mean she was *within* limits now? Did I want her to be an option? The thought itself was fine, but acting on it? I wasn't sure if I could do it.

Emma had always been a bit of an odd duck in high school. It didn't help that she fell in with the supernatural crowd without meaning to. Most humans could feel that we were different, that we were *other*, but it never bothered Emma. I'd go so far as to say that it was that *otherness* that made her feel connected to us. Perhaps that was one of the reasons I was so drawn to her, why I'd fallen for her so hard in high school even though we barely exchanged two words with each other.

She'd always been adorable, a little dorky, and the life of the party when she wanted to be. The woman I'd seen crash into a display of canned corn, though? That wasn't the Emma I knew in school and it tore at my heart that something had dimmed her light. I had to push the urge down to track down whoever had hurt her and pay them a visit.

The longer she was with her friends, though, the more the light seemed to be coming back, even if her brother was in trouble. I hoped Henry was okay. If he wasn't, then I was worried about what it might do to Emma. Her parents' death had been brutal on both of them, I knew that. I also knew that he was everything to her, and I wasn't sure but I thought that he was the only family she had left.

It had taken me so long to get over her leaving for college, for me to realize that she wasn't coming back, that she had a life elsewhere, that now that she was back, I wasn't sure how to handle it. It was only meeting Sarah that had changed my outlook on life. She saw the broken-hearted side of me and didn't care. She accepted that I'd fallen in love with a girl in high school but never talked to her. All she cared about was whether or not she and I loved each other. And we did.

So much.

Pain shot through my chest and it literally felt like my heart was breaking all over again as Sarah's face seemed to fill my mind. Just thinking about her sent shockwaves of pain through me, but they weren't nearly as bad as they used to be. Time definitely helped. The pain was still as intense, but somehow I'd grown bigger so it didn't affect me quite so much.

Emma was certainly intriguing. Maybe as a first date. I'd

been thinking about going on one. Ten years was long enough to wait, I reckoned. But nobody had caught my eye.

Except Emma.

And for some reason, I didn't think anyone would. There was just something about this woman that turned my head, always had, always would. How to go about asking her out, I had no idea. I hadn't asked a woman out since, well, I couldn't really remember doing it other than when I stumbled over my words asking Sarah out. And that was a very long time ago.

Maybe there were videos online about how to do it. I'd have to remember to check.

"Daniel!"

I sighed and turned to face the wolf pack's new, very young alpha. "Nathan."

Drawing on my inner magic, I shifted into my animal form and shook out my fur. As a bear shifter on wolf territory, this was pretty unusual, but the situation was severe. The bears usually kept to our own territories, but the wolves feared us. The pack shifted around me, snarling and snapping. But they wouldn't go on the offensive. Bears were known for their brutal attacks. The wolves might have outnumbered me, but in experience, size, and knowledge, I made up for it. I was worth ten of these pipsqueaks and they all knew it, which is why none of them advanced toward me.

It wasn't always this way. There wasn't always this tension. *Nathan, I was your father's best friend. I watched you grow up, from afar.* I mentally pushed the words at the wolf alpha. *Thomas was my best friend. His loss was a blow to us all. Whether you want to believe it or not, he was friends with all the other shifter communities in the area. This tension wasn't always there.*

Bullshit. Nathan's voice rang in my head like a bell

clanging in the distance. *I never once saw you here. You keep saying that you and Dad were friends, but there's nothing to back you up.*

My bear wanted to roar and smack the absolute shit out of him for being so dense and untrusting, but I couldn't blame him. I'd probably be the same in his shoes.

Your father, your alpha, was protective of his son. He wasn't willing to risk anything harming you. You're his heir, and he didn't want to risk a hair on that adorable little head of yours. After you were born we never met here anymore. Always off pack property, away from you, though that didn't mean your dad ever shut up about you.

He never talked about you. Nathan's voice was salty as though he was jealous of the time I spent with his father, or the fact that Thomas held his cards close to his chest. He wasn't pissed off anymore though, which was a good thing. Besides, I agreed with him on that point. The man had been so obsessed with keeping Nathan safe that he didn't think what it would be like for Nathan to be isolated from the other shifters in the area.

Nathan shook his head. His long gray fur rippled over his body as though he was standing in a gust of wind. He paced back and forth in front of me, but it was no longer aggressive; it was a man working off the adrenaline of preparing for an attack and none coming. I'd been there. Sometimes it could take a while to calm down.

Nathan shook his head, and his long gray fur began to recede as he shifted back into his skin. Watching always made me feel like I was intruding on something private, but I also knew if I turned away now it would be both an insult and make me look weak. So I watched as his skin seemed to absorb the fur that had once coated his wolf.

It happened with any shifter with fur; our bodies just

seemed to reabsorb it, just like it did with our clothes when we shifted into our animals. It creeped me out to watch though. Maybe I watched too many movies but I always wanted the clothes to shred when I shifted into my bear and the fur to turn into dust on the wind when I shifted back or something. My wallet was certainly happy that I didn't explode out of my clothes every time I shifted. Gods, could you imagine how big your closet would have to be just to keep up with yourself shifting, let alone the families with moody teenagers that shifted every two seconds? I was exhausted just thinking about it.

The young alpha stood on two legs once more after a tense moment where he was halfway between wolf and man. Another reason I was grateful we didn't lose our clothes was because I didn't want to see Nathan naked. I doubted he wanted to see me that way either.

With a sigh, he nodded once. "Fine, Bear. Why are you here?"

I shifted and strode forward, straightening my clothes as I went. "I'm looking for her brother." I nodded my head in the direction Emma had driven off.

"And I told her. I don't know where he is."

I looked him in the eyes and believed him. I believed that he didn't know where Henry was, but he had his suspicions. "Fine. What *do* you know?"

He motioned for me to sit in the chair beside him. "As I told the women, he got busted counting cards, but the Vamp Mistress made everyone let him go. My guys don't have him." He spread his hands. "As far as I know, he went home. If anyone's got him, it's the blood suckers."

That wasn't good. "Okay, thank you."

"So, you working for the department again?"

I stiffened. "Not exactly. Just still helping with the occasional supernatural case."

"I heard you were mostly just sticking to your cabin."

I almost asked if he'd had his boys watching me, but I didn't. He was still figuring this whole thing out, so if he wanted his boys to watch me, I had no issues with it. If I smelled them in my territory though, we'd have another issue altogether, just like every shifter knew. My family had been in this town as far back as anyone could remember. We still owned massive sections of the woods, even though after adulthood we were given our own territory and could only cross into each other's areas with permission.

It was a bear thing. A bear thing that every shifter, vamp, and witch alike knew.

I shrugged. "Yeah, well, a man can only do so much hunting, fishing, and reading before he gets a little bored."

There was something in his eyes I couldn't read. Did he wish wolves were like bears and that he didn't have the weight of his entire pack on his shoulders?

"Just be careful," he says. "Mystic Hollow isn't the same town as when you were in charge."

Didn't I already know that? "I appreciate it."

"And the sirens have gotten a little pushy about wanting to buy some of our land bordering the water."

My muscles tensed. "No matter the price--"

"I know. Those rich jerks can offer any price, but this is wolf land."

I released a breath I didn't know I was holding. The sirens were the most powerful, wealthy bunch in our town, but I was still shocked they even tried to buy the lands from him. Every shifter with an ounce of common sense would never sell their lands. They must have hoped he was dumb as well as inexperienced.

"Well, let me know if you have any problems with them and I'll pay them a visit."

He smirked. "I'm the alpha. I don't need anyone to intervene for me."

"Of course," I said, trying to hide my doubt.

Sighing, I rubbed my hand across my face and looked around. The wolf pack, now that they knew I wasn't a threat, went back to whatever they'd been doing when I drove up.

I furrowed my brow. Which was, apparently, cleaning. Black trash bags were stacked by the meeting house, and some of the younger wolves were scrubbing paint off the side of a house. "What's going on? The houses are looking rough up here."

Nathan chuckled, but the sound was sad, not amused. "I know my dad was a better alpha. There have been a lot of issues with the shifters, but I'm trying." He met my gaze. "I really am."

"Can I help?" I knew he'd turn me down, but I had to try, not just because he was Thomas's kid, but because he was good at his core. I knew that he would be a fair, strong alpha; it was within him. He deserved having all the help he wanted or needed.

As expected, he shook his head.

I sighed and smiled at him. "You're very much like your father, Nathan. If he'd lived longer…"

Nathan's eyes moistened, and he cleared his throat. "Well, he didn't. Now, I have to do the best I can with what I have."

If his father had lived, the boy could've been molded into an incredible alpha. He had a lot of growing to do, but I had to be careful. Too much advice or given the wrong way and he would shut me out completely.

Standing, I held out my hand. "Please, Nathan. If you

ever need anything, don't hesitate. I loved your father very much. I'm here for you."

Nathan shook my hand and looked me in the eye like a man. He would grow into his position and learn from mistakes. I just hoped those mistakes didn't hurt too much.

I turned and returned to my car. Sitting there for a moment, I looked out at the wolf's camp. I spent many days and nights there with Thomas before he became a father. We were eerily similar to the wolves I saw in front of me now, or at least I suspected so. Drinking around the bonfire, seducing shifter females with no idea if one of them might turn out to be our mate and end our bachelor shenanigans. I would be willing to bet that they went cliff diving just like we used to. For just a moment I could almost see a young Thomas moving among them.

It was easy to feel invincible when you were that age. Adults, but just barely, most with no real responsibilities yet, just out to have a good time. Once you lost someone, though? You realized how fragile we all were even if we were shifters.

As I looked around, I realized that this was no longer a safe place for me, however, and these wolves were no longer my friends. They may never be, at least not to the degree that Thomas was, and that was okay. Things evolved, changed. They had to.

Off in the distance, there was a boom and a slight shaking of the ground. I sighed and leaned back in my chair. I'd have to remind the dwarves to be cautious with their mining. There was a lot we could explain away to the humans, but we supernaturals still couldn't be reckless.

I turned on my car and drove off the pack lands, heading toward my cabin at the edge of town. Already, my warm fire and slowly cooking chili were waiting. That was one thing the boy hadn't been wrong about; I did spend a lot of my time home. Bears were naturally homebodies, but with a case to focus on, and the mysterious Emma back in town, I finally had a reason to spend more time around society.

Which might not be a bad thing.

Now, I just had to wait until nightfall. Time to see the vampires.

12

Ugh. I'd forgotten about the mess.

Deva had dropped me off at my house. It was nowhere near nightfall, the late afternoon sun mocking me, and therefore there wasn't much we could do until we could talk to the vampires. Deva had to go deal with some stuff at her restaurant, and Carol had claimed she needed to open the store for at least a little bit.

With a sigh, I hung my purse on the hall tree and picked up a picture with the glass cracked right down the middle. It was of my brother with our parents. I could almost remember that day. We had gone to a cider mill and picked some apples from their orchard. Henry had been happy because they were fresh and crunchy. The sky had been a brilliantly clear blue which made the fall leaves look even brighter against it in the background. My heart panged thinking about our mom and dad.

The accident had been horrific. Sometimes I could feel the shattered glass under my hands and feet as I crawled out, and saw my parents crumpled in front seats. No child should have to see something like that. I knew death was unavoidable, I had my whole life since we lost my grandparents while I was still young, but someone dying versus being turned into mush by one of those oversized pickup trucks were two different things.

The funeral had been overwhelming. That's what happens when you live in a small town and everyone knows everyone else. Henry had locked himself in his room and just getting him to come to the ceremony had been a battle in and of itself, so when he did the same with the wake, I let him. Which meant it was me and the whole town. Everyone wanting to comfort me, and none of them being able to.

At the time, I'd felt like I was drifting alone on a sea of black. Black suits. Black dresses. Black hats. Black veils. Yes, some of the mourners were that dramatic. All of it punctuated by the white of the lilies that everyone brought. As if I needed flowers in that moment.

The food, on the other hand, was much appreciated.

It wasn't that I couldn't cook, that was something Mom had insisted that we both learn, but neither of us had the motivation to do anything other than call for takeout or heat up leftovers.

I pushed the memories away, knowing that this was a dangerous road to go down at the best of times, and with Henry missing and in trouble, I'd hardly call this the best of times. Swallowing thickly, I tried to focus on the present, but all that seemed to want to invade my thoughts was the past. I tried to sweep them from my mind by focusing on cleaning.

Righting a small table, I grabbed the rest of the picture frames that had rested on it. They'd survived without the glass breaking, somehow. As I positioned them on the table again, a picture of my son and ex-husband caught my eye.

Gross. Now I was stuck thinking about Rick and his

froggy-went-a-courtin. I giggled and swiped at the tears on my face. What was I going to do about him being a frog, or toad, or whatever? It wasn't like I'd turned into a witch that could do—or undo—spells. And even if I could, how would I find the right two toads in the garden? What if they'd hopped home? They could be anywhere in the world by now. Well, that might be a slight exaggeration, but they could certainly be far enough away from our old house that I didn't stand a chance of finding them.

Stumbling forward, I sank slowly down on the sofa as my breathing shallowed and panic gripped my throat. I stared at the picture of my son with his father and began to cry in earnest, sobs wracking my body. This wasn't a pretty cry. There was no dabbing daintily at my eyes with a hand-kerchief, oh, no. This was full-blown hiccuping, snot-bubble-forming, drooling crying. It was the kind of thing I could only let loose when I was alone.

This whole karma thing was fun, but I'd turned my son's father into a toad. Then, instead of keeping track of him, left him outside. He was probably literally slimy now. Hopping around croaking at all the lady frogs or toads. I hoped they all ignored him.

A bubble of laughter warred with my tears, because damn if he hadn't deserved it. It was that thought that finally had the sobs subsiding. I couldn't decide if I felt guilty or relieved, but as I wrestled with my emotions, my phone rang in my pocket, a song I'd set just to mean Travis was calling.

Digging in my pants, I pulled the phone out, and nearly burst into another wave of tears when I saw the photo of my son on my lock screen. I took a few deep breaths to try to get the tears out of my voice, swallowing hard as I hit the speaker button, then set the phone beside me on the sofa. "Hey, buddy. What's going on?"

"You okay, Mom? I just felt like I needed to talk to you all of a sudden."

I sighed and opened the back of the frame with the picture of Travis and Rick in it. "I was having a moment. It's like you called at the perfect time. You okay?"

"Yeah, I just got home to do some laundry. Where are you?"

I could almost see him wandering around the house, laundry spilling out of the bag he used since he waited too long to do it. I knew he'd have to go back through the house, picking up socks here and there, grabbing armfuls of t-shirts off the floor, and once he had it all together, I was sure he would overfill the washer. Part of me was embarrassed by the state that I'd left the house in, but he was my son. He knew my heart had been broken by his father, so if anyone was going to cut me some slack, it would be the kid that would bring armfuls of dirty glasses down from his room.

Thinking about it all made my heart ache from missing him. He was more than I ever expected when I found out I was pregnant. Everything about him amazed me. How I'd helped create this human being who was so kind and smart and decent, especially when he had Rick for a father, I'd never know, but would forever be grateful for.

The click of the dial on the washer drew me back from my thoughts. "I actually decided to come back to Mystic Hollow to see Henry and take a little break from reality." That hadn't worked out so well. Reality had kinda freaked out on me. "You okay there?" *Have you seen any crazy toads jumping around?*

"Yeah, but I had wanted to talk to you while I was here." There was something in his voice akin to apprehension that made my stomach twist.

I banished anything except gentle curiosity from my voice as I said, "About what, Pumpkin?"

"I had dinner with Dad and Candy the other night. It was really awkward."

I just bet it was. She was closer to his age than Rick's. "It will be that way, especially at first. Just like any new experience can be at first." I'd tried *really* hard through all this not to bad mouth Rick to our son. He was still his father and I wouldn't have Travis resent Rick on my part. If that happened, it had to be all Travis's emotions driving it, not my voice in his head telling him what to think or feel.

Knowing Rick, I was certain he would eventually drive his son away just by how he would favor Candy over Travis. No one liked being picked last for the dodgeball team, and Rick was king of avoiding the people he considered less than himself. With Candy buoying him, I knew he'd see Travis as something he didn't need to bother with any more since he'd never really been interested in having kids in the first place.

"No, it was more than that. It was like Candy was *jealous* of me. I really can't stand her."

"Oh, no. I'm sorry, honey." *Do not cackle like a madwoman. Do not cackle like a madwoman. Hold it together, Emma.* Of course I was sad that the dinner hadn't gone well and Travis hadn't had a good time, but part of me, an embarrassingly large part, wanted Travis to have nothing to do with Rick and Candy.

"Dad didn't even notice. I just don't think I want to have anything to do with them anymore."

No happy dances. This isn't a competition. I cleared my throat so I didn't sound overly happy at his statement. "You know I'll support you, whatever you decide. But he's your father. Don't close the door completely." Even though I didn't want him spending a lot of time with Rick and Candy, I couldn't help but remind my son that having a father was not something he should throw away. He didn't have to vacation with them, and he couldn't really since they were now toads, or frogs, or whatever, but he shouldn't burn that bridge, no matter how much I wanted to hand him the gasoline and a lighter.

After all, you never know when you might want a pet frog.

"Okay, maybe, but I do think I'm going to take a step back from him for a while. My engineering classes are harder than I thought, and I just want to be able to focus on them."

Good. That might buy me some time to figure out the toad-thing. "That sounds like a good plan. So, how's everything else?"

He huffed a little, and I could imagine him going back through the house, picking up his stray socks. "Becca and I are still doing well. We're both on track to graduate next year, and then we're talking about where we're going to go from there."

We're. My baby had a woman he spoke about in the we form. Ever since I'd met Becca, an outgoing, lovely girl going to school to become a teacher, I'd loved her. She was like the daughter I'd never had, but I tried to keep my thoughts to myself. My son was still young enough that he didn't need that kind of pressure. But now, hearing him talk about what they'd be doing after school made that little flicker of excitement inside of me grow.

"That's exciting!" I said, then tried to calm my voice. "Any ideas so far?"

"Actually..." He hesitated. "I was telling her a little about Mystic Hollow. I hadn't known you'd gone back at the time, but she was saying that moving to a small town near the ocean might be a lot of fun. Are you planning on staying?"

For a second I imagined them here and my lips curled into a smile. "I'm thinking about it. The only thing really tying me back there now is you."

"Well." I could hear a smile in his own voice. "Don't make any plans because of me. Becca and I don't want to stay local no matter what."

It was strange. My son was really growing up. "I've never really chosen anything just because I wanted it." The words left my mouth before I realized it.

"I know, Mom. But I'm in college, Dad is being Dad, what better time could you choose something just for you?"

He was right. "How in the world did we raise such an awesome person?"

"You raised an awesome person," he said. "Dad drifted in every once and awhile."

He wasn't wrong. "Well, I'm lucky to have you."

"Love you, Mom."

"I love you, too, Pumpkin." Ugh. I wanted to give him a hug so badly in that moment.

"Well, better start the laundry and kill some time studying."

"Okay, bye."

"Bye," he said, his voice so damn sweet to hear.

I ended the call and stared at my phone, suddenly weary to my very bones. Today felt like it had lasted forever. Too many things had happened. Henry was still missing and I didn't feel any closer to finding him if I was honest, which sent another wave of emotion through me and had me wanting to curl up into a ball and not face the world anymore. I mean, what more did it want me to give?

I'd opened the back of the frame, so I slid out the photo

and looked at Rick. Stupid emotions. When would they calm down? While another tear snaked down my cheek, I ripped the photo in half, keeping the half with Travis on it in my hand and letting the half of the picture with Rick on it float down to the floor with the broken glass. Then, I put the picture of my parents and brother in the unbroken frame and stuck Travis in there, too, arranging it so I could see all of them. They were a little squished but it worked.

After unpacking the groceries from my car and putting what was salvageable away, I went and set the photo of my family on the nightstand, and collapsed on the bed, staring at the photo until sleep claimed me. Those four people meant the world to me, even if two of them were gone from this world. I would not let a third go, not this soon, not before his time, no matter what.

I would save Henry. I had no choice. Not if I wanted to live with myself.

13

EMMA

"**W**ake up."

I sat bolt upright in bed and slowly turned my head to the window. The sun was low in the sky, glowing in that golden way it did in autumn, and a pretty damn big blackbird perched on the windowsill. It's feathers gleamed in the low light.

And it stared at me, its beady eyes seeing too much as it tilted its head to the side as though it needed to get a better view.

"Hello?" Had I dreamt the call to wake up?

"Wake up," it croaked.

Nope. Definitely real. "I'm awake," I whispered.

The bird tilted its head again and let out a normal-sounding caw, then flew away just as my phone vibrated on the bed beside my butt, faintly jiggling the softness of my body that was there. "Oh, shoot," I muttered and grabbed it. "Hello?"

"I've been calling you for like an hour. Did my bird come?" Beth said by way of greeting.

"Sorry! I fell asleep. I'm not sure why my phone is on

vibrate." I put it on speaker, then checked the button on the side. "I must've hit the button to switch it to silent mode." That was a problem with this brand of phone.

"It's fine, but you don't have much time. There's food on its way to you from Deva's restaurant. Eat it, get ready, and I'll pick you up at ten."

"Wait, why? What?"

"We're going to the club, and my agency is helping you find Henry." She sounded so proud that it made my heart fill with happiness for her. She had built her agency from nothing. It was her thing and no one could take it from her, especially not cheating ex-partners.

"What about Deva and Carol?"

"Carol's employee called in sick tonight, so she has to cover the fabric store, and Deva still does a couple dinner shifts a week. She has that fancy chef of hers, so she can have a life, but she still loves the rush of actually running a shift, rather than just baking pies and pastries in the mornings."

"Oh, okay," I whispered, already feeling like I should just stay in bed, like my body was going to be angry at me for whatever it was I was about to do. I glanced down at the time and saw how late it was already.

"Isn't ten a little late?" I felt dumb. Should I have been up earlier?

Beth laughed in my ear, a pure, joyful sound. "Stop acting like such a forty-year-old." She snorted in amusement.

"Beth, honey, we *are* forty-year-olds." And then some.

"Well, I know, but we don't have to act like it. People are just getting going at ten. It's kind of early for where we're going. Just be ready to go." She wasn't about to back down and I wasn't about to turn down her help.

"Okay," I said as a twinkling chime filled the air. "Doorbell. Food must be here."

"See you at ten!"

I hurried to the front door, digging in my purse for some cash for the tip. I only had a few bills, which I hoped would be a decent enough tip for a delivery guy. Then I checked my phone and realized I'd slept all evening and it really wasn't that far from ten now. I needed to hurry. That long, hot shower I'd been planning to get ready certainly wasn't going to happen. I'd be lucky if I got to eat a few mouthfuls of food and run a comb through my hair.

After an awkward interaction with the delivery driver, I made my way back to the center of the house. Ignoring the mess in the living room that I'd never really cleaned up, I hurried into the kitchen and grabbed a bottle of water and fork. Then, glancing around, I decided to go out on the back patio and have my dinner there.

Setting it all down on the little table, I glanced at the beach and spotted a young man walking alone. He had a trash bag in one hand and was wearing gloves. Every so often he bent down and grabbed something, then dropped it in the bag. As I watched him, I realized he was cleaning up the beach. Something warm and pleasant moved through me, and I swear I felt a wave rush out of me. He suddenly stiffened and looked in my direction. I held my breath, and then he kept going.

Karma. How had I forgotten karma could bring the good with the bad? I didn't know exactly how karma would reward the kid, but I knew it would. And it was strange. In that moment, after living a lifetime wanting to know deep down that good things could happen to good people, I now had a role in that. It made me proud of my powers for the first time.

I sighed and looked down at the table. No more time to waste if I wanted to eat. And I *really* wanted to eat. Unpacking the food, I moaned in delight. Just the smell of whatever was in the box was enough to have my mouth watering and my stomach growling.

I swallowed a mouthful of drool and cracked open the box. A bowl of rigatoni sat inside, the noodles covered in a creamy-looking sauce that had my mouth watering all over again, not to mention the kale and sausage that were mixed in.

My fork dove into the dish as though it had a mind of its own, but I knew it was just that I was hungry enough that shoveling food into my mouth was the last thing I was going to be embarrassed about. I speared a few noodles and a bit of kale and popped it in my mouth, having to breathe in because it was still so hot that it was scalding my tongue. The creamy, pumpkiny, tomatoey sauce was luxurious, so much so that I groaned out loud and looked down at my food bowl with skepticism. Was I imagining how good this was?

Doubtful.

Deva was just that good.

I should never have let so much time pass between eating meals she made.

The next forkful delivered a few more noodles and this time I could taste the touch of sage and browned butter in the sauce. Damn, this woman was good. She should go on Iron Chef or something. Did that show even still exist? I'd loved it but Rick had hated it, said that it took no talent to cook, which was why I did all the cooking. He certainly didn't have the talent for it.

Bite after bite filled me with a delicious sense of fullness and soon enough the bowl was empty.

After cramming the to-go container in the garbage can, I went to see what I had to wear. I wasn't exactly excited about the choices that awaited me.

I hadn't brought a single thing with me that was appropriate for wearing to a club, unless mom jeans and a v-neck tee were club outfits these days. Wouldn't that be nice? Let women be comfy when they go out. Who wants to stuff themselves into spiked heels and tight dresses with our hair and makeup done to hell and back? Couldn't we just wear whatever we wanted, throw our hair up in a messy bun, and call it done? I mean, that's what they would get eventually anyway. We're all just deceiving ourselves if we expect to be picture perfect all the time. Would Beth still take me to the club in my mom jeans?

Somehow I doubted it.

I didn't even check my bags, knowing there was nothing waiting for me in there. Wincing, I opened my closet door.

As I'd suspected. It was mostly empty. I slid the few hangers from one side to the other. After our parents funeral we had donated most of their clothing, except for a few pieces we couldn't stand to part with. That wasn't my goal, though. No way was I wearing one of my mom's old dresses, unless it was retro night or something, and even then I wouldn't want to risk it. We held on to them because of sentimental reasons, which meant I wasn't about to accidentally wreck it just because I needed something to wear to a vampire club.

No, my goal was the few things that I'd left behind, ones that Henry had moved in here when he converted my old bedroom. The first thing that caught my eye was my high school cheerleading outfit. There was the bridesmaids dress I'd worn at Deva's wedding, a few old pairs of jeans that I loved and had decorated myself with patches and embroidery, and a couple flowy, summery skirts that I'd thought were the coolest thing when I bought them, although seeing at them now I probably looked like I belonged at some kind of commune. Then, at the back, behind my high school graduation robe, a slinky black dress. I was surprised I'd even left it, but it had blended in with the dark fabric of my robe. If I hadn't noticed the final hanger hook then I probably wouldn't have looked any further.

There was no way this thing was fitting. I was a good twenty pounds heavier, and it was only a little bit in the boobs.

But it was literally the only appropriate thing to wear, so I tried it.

Oh, damn. What about shoes?

When it came to shoes, I knew I had too many but I couldn't help it. They were so pretty and there were so many different styles. It was because of how many I had, and therefore had packed, that I thought I may actually have something appropriate to wear. I grabbed my suitcase and rifled through, grinning triumphantly when my fingers slid over some familiar black leather. I'd brought low-heeled, black ankle boots. They'd work great. See, the thing was, even though I had a bunch of shoes, I only ever wore a few pairs. I saved the others for just the right occasion, which never really came.

Ten minutes later, I had my hair in a high ponytail and a couple of layers of mascara on, some shiny lip gloss, and was ready to step out front with my phone and debit card and ID in my bra to wait for Beth. It was nearly ten, anyway.

Standing awkwardly, I tugged at my dress. I couldn't believe this thing had fit after all these years. It was a good thing it was so damn stretchy.

Spandex was very forgiving, and it wrinkled in the right

places to hide the small belly pouch I still carried all these years later from having Travis. Not that I'd trade it for the world.

I heard Beth coming before she pulled up. When she drove into the driveway, I realized why. She was in a bright red convertible with the top down, blaring pop music from our high school and college years.

Oh, blast from the past, hello. I hurried around the car and slid into the passenger seat. "Hey, hon!" I called over the music. "Our youth called. It wants to go to bed."

She burst out laughing and backed out of the driveway as I yawned for the first time, but not the last.

The songs effortlessly wove in and out of one another, dredging up all kinds of memories. The song that everyone was obsessed with our senior year came on and I burst out laughing.

"I can't believe you have this on a playlist. Didn't you get sick of it?" I asked, faux surprise on my face as I secretly loved listening to it again.

Beth grinned. "I mean, yeah, but it's good to reminisce. Remember when Charlie fell on her ass carrying her lunch and ended up covered in chocolate milk and tomato soup? This was playing on that stereo the popular kids had. See? Memories."

"Oh, remember when Jimmy and Kristen got written up for dancing too provocatively to this at the homecoming dance?" I gasped, the memory coming out of nowhere. I hadn't thought about either of them in decades.

"Detention for a week! How could I forget that? Biggest scandal of the year!"

The song changed to one that was slightly more obscure. "Oh, I bet you don't remember all the lyrics to this one," I said, daring her.

"Please! I know these songs from front to back," Beth said a second before she jumped in on the lyrics, singing along flawlessly.

Her enthusiasm was such that I couldn't help but join in. The wind whipped my hair around and I lifted my hands, letting the air rush over my skin as I felt the joy at simply being with one of my best friends and singing songs we grew up with fill my heart. We used to do the same thing back in the day. Drive around, sing songs, gossip. For a moment, I flashed back to us as teenagers and wondered what my teen self would think of my adult self. Whatever it was I didn't care. I was happy. It may have just been for a few minutes, but I was truly happy. It had been much longer than I cared to admit since I felt this way. This relaxed, this much myself.

I sang at the top of my lungs until Beth pulled off the road and into a parking lot. It was pretty much the only club in town, considering we were barely big enough for a second grocery store. The concrete and metal facade had a bit of an ultra modern look to it. All sharp angles and rectangles.

It looked like every twenty-something in town was here, based on the line at the door. "This doesn't look like a vampire club," I said when Beth shut off the engine.

She grinned at me. "Just you wait."

14

EMMA

The line took an eternity, or at least that's what it felt like. Figuring we'd been standing here at least an hour, I checked my phone, and it had only been about ten minutes. Shit. It was awkward standing with all these young people, each of them looking like they could be hanging out with my son. The guys trying to look suave and badass at the same time while the girls were tittering with each other in dresses that were crazy short and heels that would have given me vertigo.

Those ten minutes passed like ten hours.

Each one dragged like the last class of the school day.

Beth kept up a steady stream of conversation with me barely participating, too distracted by everything around me and the prospect of entering a vampire club. She didn't seem to mind too much, though, as she filled me in on what everyone from our high school was doing now. How many kids each of the popular crowd had now, and how many marriages they'd been through. I felt a pang of disappointment that I would now be in the list of divorced members of our high school class. Honestly, the thought of getting married again was exhausting. I didn't know if it was for me.

Daniel's face flashed in my mind, his jade green eyes pinning me with his stare.

Nope.

Not going there.

He might be pretty to look at, and I might have crushed on him super hard in high school, but my heart wasn't ready for anything just yet. I wasn't sure if it ever would be. How did I learn to trust again when the person I trusted most in the world just betrayed me in every way imaginable?

I looked at my surroundings, forcing myself to focus on the present. Beth's voice was soothing in my ear, and I tried to listen to what she was saying, I really did, but my mind drifted. I couldn't help but wonder if some of these people knew what they were walking into.

How many of them thought they were going to get sparkly vampires and how many thought they were going to get men in long black capes? Were either of them even accurate for that matter? I certainly had no idea.

Were some of them hoping to be bitten? Was that even how you became a vampire? Or did they just like the idea of feeding a vampire? I really needed to find out some of these basic details before we left for an exclusive club next time.

Eventually, it was our turn at the front. The bouncer turned from letting two giggly girls into the club, who were surprisingly adept on stripper heels with their thongs practically hanging out, and looked down at us. He laughed out loud and shook his head. "No way. Come on." He turned and looked at the two guys standing on either side of the door. "Are you guys punking me?"

They shook their heads and looked at Beth and I in

amusement. Their lips quirked up just a little at one corner, each one a mirror of the other.

"What does that mean?" I asked.

The bouncer looked down at us again, and I caught a glimpse of fang. Oh, shit. He was a vampire. "You're old."

I bet you're older if you're a vampire, I thought, not that I'd ever say it out loud. I took a step, preparing to turn and leave empty handed, but Beth had other ideas.

"Excuse me?" she hissed as she stepped forward and looked up. The giant of a man—vampire—didn't flinch. And honestly, a cute witch versus a bodybuilding vampire that looked like he should be on the cover of a romance novel? Why would he? Beth practically growled as she demanded, "Did you just say *old*?"

He didn't move, but somehow he seemed bigger and more threatening as he glared down at Beth. His bulk looked like it was growing in my line of sight, though I was sure that wasn't what was happening. He was probably just flexing, beefing himself up to get Beth to back down. I was certainly willing to back down and leave since I couldn't help but think of how he could smush us like bugs.

"Hey, let's just go," I whispered. "We don't want to piss these guys off."

But the main bouncer wasn't having it. "Take these two grandmas into the back and teach them a lesson about respect," he said in a voice so low I wasn't sure the other two could hear it.

They must've, though, because they stepped forward. I stepped back, ready to run for the car with a scream building in my throat, but once they were close to grabbing her, Beth raised her hand and threw some sort of powder into all three of their faces. The white cloud started small, erupting from her hand like a volcano, and as it reached them it turned shimmery in the spotlight that shone above the door. It only lasted for a moment before the powder vanished completely.

The enormous men blinked rapidly, and one of them sneezed. The burst of noise seemed to shake them from their stupor, then they all shook their heads in unison. "Let us in," Beth said in a low voice.

The bouncer nodded and stepped back, and his two goons went to their positions at the door, one of them reaching over and opening it as Beth and I walked in.

Well, Beth *strutted* in like she owned the place. I looked behind me to see if any of the kids had noticed, but no one had even glanced in our direction. Was this a witch thing? Could humans not see what we did? I'd have to ask later. For now, I needed to follow Beth, who was evidently pleased with getting her way. I, on the other hand, more scurried and cowered as I made my way through the doors.

And as soon as I stepped foot inside, I slammed straight into someone's back. "Oh, I'm sorry," I said, but the music was too loud.

The woman and her friends, the ones who had been in line ahead of us, turned and leered. She looked me over, then Beth, her lip curling upward in a sneer. "Old bitch." I couldn't hear her, but her lips weren't hard to read.

One of the others looked at Beth and just as I glanced her way, I saw her mouth move. "Fatass."

Oh, hell, no. Vampires were one thing, but no way I was letting this child get away with calling my friend fat.

Almost in unison, the three of them clutched their stomachs. Their brows all pinched in a familiar way, one that said trouble was on the horizon. The music stopped, and as it always was in places like this when the loud song was over, the silence deafened for a moment. But another song didn't immediately come on, so when the one who called Beth a fatass farted, it was like an echo, ricocheting across the club.

Her friends stared at her in shock, but then one of them doubled over and moaned. Suddenly, as my gaze shifted to the people behind them, I realized that everyone was looking in this direction. Their gazes focused on the girls in front of us as the three of them and their butts started sounding like trumpets. Little honks, and big, flapping claps of ass cheeks, and not in the sexy dancer way either. These were high-pitched whines. Combine that with the moans that were coming from them? They were a cacophony of noise.

As though they couldn't stand the horror on everyone's faces any longer, the girls ran toward what I assumed was a bathroom, or who knows? Maybe it was just a closet. It seemed like they would go anywhere so long as it got them out of the spotlight.

I really hoped it was a bathroom for the sake of the cleaning crew. The one that had called us old had a distinctive brown trail running down the inside and back of her legs as she waddled through the doorway. The sour notes that had been on the air were finally cut off as the door closed behind them.

The moment it did, everyone around us burst out laughing. The few people that were closest to us had tears running down their faces as they doubled over with laughter. I couldn't help but wonder if the tears were actually from the laughter or from the smell that was still lingering in the air.

I stared at them all, shock brimming within me. Had I done that?

Before I could ask Beth, the music finally came back

with a blaring beat, drowning out their next words. The pause had been much too long. No DJ would ever allow something like that, so either someone was screwing up or this was a playlist with no one manning it, or worse, I'd caused the music to pause as well so that the girls could be sufficiently mortified by their gastric distress.

A moment later, before we could step away, the girls came out of the bathroom. One of them had toilet paper clinging to the bottom of her high heels like a bride's train. They quickly pushed past us toward the door we'd all just come in, and I couldn't wipe the grin off my face.

They glared at us as they passed, and I didn't really need to hear their words. I knew what was going on.

"What did you do?" Beth yelled in my ear.

I leaned over and put my mouth next to her ear as I yelled back, "I have no idea! How did you get us in?"

She moved back over and put her mouth next to my head, but she didn't yell. "Magic," her voice whispered in my ear, as if we were in a silent room. Chills erupted over my skin and a shiver zinged down my spine.

Grinning, I shook my head at her. "You're amazing!" I shouted.

Beth either heard me or got my meaning, because she smiled and grabbed my hand as she started working her way through the crowd toward the bar. The whole thing was shocking, and hilarious, but I still wasn't sure why we were here. Despite the vampires at the door, this place seemed to be full of humans. Not vampires. Or shifters.

I tugged on Beth's arm and leaned close. "Nothing about this place seems out of the ordinary," I yelled in her ear, careful about exactly what I said since I didn't really know for sure these were all humans.

Her voice whispered in my ear again, even though she

was nowhere near close enough for me to hear her, yet hear her I did. "Looks can be deceiving." She tossed me a wink before adding, "This is just the front. We have to go downstairs for the real fun."

Oh, boy. I wasn't sure I was ready for the *real* fun.

Downstairs.

15

EMMA

Beth pulled me into a quiet corner, and I stared out at the room packed with people. Different colored lights flashed overhead and the bass was so strong it seemed to shake the ground. I tried to remember if clubs were the same when I used to go to them in college, but everything seemed brighter and louder now.

But also not like a vampire den.

"So what's the plan?" I asked, frowning as I continued scanning the room.

"We go downstairs, ask about your brother, and hopefully explain that this has all been a big misunderstanding and get him back," she said, like it was the simplest thing in the world.

"Do you think it'll be so easy?" I didn't know a thing about vampires.

She lifted a brow. "Not a chance. But the thing is, supernaturals aren't just bloodthirsty monsters. We have codes. If the vampires just completely disregard a witch's request, they risk pissing us all off, and we're a powerful group. But they're not just going to give him up. There's probably going to be a price, so we need to be ready for that."

A price? I took a deep breath. Whatever it was, I'd find a way to pay it.

"Okay." I released my breath.

"Ready to take on a room full of arrogant vampires?" she asked, studying me.

No, I was not. "I need a little courage first," I admitted. "The liquid kind."

Beth nodded earnestly. "I feel that. Really do. Liquid courage has given me the strength to do a lot of things I never imagined this past year."

There was no way that Beth had done so much just because of liquid courage.

I couldn't help but stare at her a little. Beth really amazed me. Even though our situations were so similar, she seemed so *over* her cheating ex, unlike me. She'd been with her ex for nearly twenty years, about as long as I was married. I'd never officially met the guy. Apparently, he was one of the few people who moved from another place to Mystic Hollow, without any ties to the place. But she'd told me enough in our phone calls to know he'd been cheating on her with a younger woman too. She didn't speak about it often. I assumed it was because it'd hurt too much to discuss, but was it really just that she'd found a way to come to terms with it?

I didn't have a clue.

But her confident air, and the way she seemed so at home here, made me think maybe she was just doing well. The thought made me happy as she spun on her heel and started pushing through the crowd. It was good that at least one of us had it together.

We headed straight for the bar. "Four shots of your top shelf whiskey," she shouted and slapped down a fifty. "Keep the change!"

I raised my eyebrows, but she shrugged. "The drinks are ten dollars apiece anyway. It's just a tenner for him," she said in my ear.

The bartender nodded and pulled out a stack of shot glasses, the squat, round glasses dripping with moisture as though they'd just been washed. There were plenty of people in the club so it wouldn't surprise me if they were cleaning glasses as fast as people were using them. The large bottle he grabbed from the top shelf behind the bar was already half empty and the liquid inside sloshed around a second before he flipped it upside down over the first shot glass.

As soon as that one was full, he moved to the next, raising and lowering the bottle over each consecutive glass. I knew it was a trick of the eye, something bartenders did to make it seem like they were pouring more when in fact they were all the same amount. He pushed the tiny glasses toward us and spread them out between the two of us.

We each picked up a glass, clinking them together before tapping the bottom on the bar and raising them to our lips, letting the fiery burn of the whiskey work its magic as we each downed our first one then, after a second quick cheers, the second. My whole body felt like it was being warmed from the inside out.

Rick didn't like whiskey and I'd forgotten how much I enjoyed it. He only ever drank vodka or rum. Sure, they were good, but whiskey and I got along like a house on fire.

"Good?" she asked.

I grinned, and I couldn't seem to wipe the grin off my

face. "Better than good. Do you have any idea how awesome you are?"

She laughed. "Are you drunk already? Emma, you need to get out more! Live a little!"

"No, seriously, you're awesome. I wish I had half your confidence."

Her smile wavered, then was back. "You'll get there. I promise."

I shook my head. "I was never like you. I was--"

"Awesome in your own way. I remember the way you could sing when you thought no one was around. You have the most incredible voice I've ever heard."

I swallowed around the lump in my throat. "That was all my mom. She had wanted to be a famous singer, but then she got pregnant with me, and she decided to stay in Mystic Hollow. But she never forgot what it felt like to be on a stage. We'd stand out on the back patio and sing together, even though only the birds were listening."

"I remember your mom," Beth said, and her smile turned to a sad one. "She was an incredible woman."

We ordered another shot. I wanted to chase that warm feeling again, not think about my mom turning up the stereo and us belting out songs together. Nor about my dad building Legos with Henry. Those two had covered the living room in Lego sets that no one dared to touch until after the funeral, when Henry took them apart piece-by-piece, tears streaming down his face.

He hadn't cried at the funeral. He *did* cry then. And when he tossed those boxes of Legos in the trash, we'd both aged years.

Damn it. I grabbed my shot and raised it to Beth.

She spoke, her voice strong and sure. "To every valley we had to overcome to reach the top of this hill."

I clinked my glass with hers and downed another drink. The warmth inside of me grew hotter, pleasantly so, and my thoughts scattered. Beth was right. We'd been through a lot. Saving Henry? We would do this too, and no one was going to stop us.

"Let's do this!" I yelled when all the glasses sat empty in front of us.

Beth pointed to a door toward the back of the club. "That's where we have to go!"

"Then that's where we're going!"

Steeling my shoulders and spine, I marched over to a bouncer guarding a door. It didn't look like the rest of the wall, which surprised me, since I thought it would have been more subtle. Instead, it was tufted black leather, looking luxurious and dangerous all at once. I'd even seen people slipping through while we had our drinks. This was the way to the downstairs. I was sure of it.

"Excuse me," I shouted.

He glanced down without actually moving his head and arched one eyebrow. "Yes?" His deep voice vibrated through my body like Lurch from the Addams family.

I cocked my hip and tossed my hair over my shoulder. Out of the corner of my eye, I saw the ends of my hair slap Beth in the eye.

Oh, damn.

Ignoring her flinches and movements behind me, I tried to look up coyly at the man. "How are you?"

He finally moved his head to look down at me, his dark eyes raking over my face as though trying to figure out what I was up to. "Fine."

"A man of few words, eh?" I asked. "I like that."

Sucking in a deep breath, I managed to choke on air and stray spit and had to turn away, so I could hack up a lung without it being right in the bouncer's face. The next thing I knew, Lurch was pounding on my back so hard I was afraid that the hacking up a lung thing would actually happen. His large hand smacked against my back again as I finally got myself under control.

"Are you okay?"

Oh, geez. His voice never rose in tone. It stayed that deep, flat intonation that resonated.

Pulling myself upright, I wheezed through a raw throat. "I'm fine."

Wow, he actually seemed concerned. Go Lurch. He'd liked my flirting. Excellent. "So, I'm looking for my brother, Henry. Do you know him? He's good at cards."

Lurch froze and pressed at his ear. I hadn't even noticed he was wearing an earpiece until that moment, and I wasn't sure I'd have been able to tell if it wasn't for the tiny cord that appeared from behind his ear and disappeared around his neck. He turned his head away from me so I couldn't hear what he said, but the vibrations of his voice were apparent, like hearing the bass line of a song but not the lyrics. He was talking to someone.

A few seconds later, the black leather door behind him opened and two men walked out, fangs peeking through their lips. There was something about the vamps that sent a chill down my spine even with the whiskey warming my belly. It was as if my instincts were screaming that these creatures could seriously hurt me.

In any other life, at any other time, I don't think I could have faced them. But I was Henry's protector. I always had been. Today wasn't any different.

"This way," one of them said.

And even though I was scared out of my mind, I straightened my spine. Scary vampires or not, I was going to get my brother back. God protect anyone who gets in my way.

Lurch winked at me as I passed him, the gesture oddly animated for a man who had barely even raised his eyebrow earlier. "Have fun," he drolled.

Beth and I followed the vampires, practically glued at the hip.

"So, you've been down here before?" I whispered to Beth.

She made a little sound. "Not *exactly*, but I have heard a lot about it."

Oh man, that was not what I wanted to hear. Beth seemed so confident about tonight. It sounded like she came here every other weekend. But then again, it probably would've been smarter for me to have asked her rather than just assuming it.

But rather than entering some creepy serial killer's basement, we found ourselves on stairs that were well lit, with wooden walls that the woman from the home and garden channel would've loved. Ship-something decor. I didn't have a clue. I wanted to ask Beth more about what she heard about the vampires and this part of the club, but I figured it wasn't a good idea, with the bouncers a few feet in front of us.

Once we got downstairs, I stopped in shock at what I was seeing. The stairs had seemed to last longer than I'd expected and now I understood why. The first thing I noticed was how the air had changed. It didn't have that sweaty alcohol and sex smell that the club had upstairs. It was cooler, fresher.

It was like an old-school speakeasy. There were large oval tables that were surrounded by leather booths at the entrance then as the room opened up it became almost a hodgepodge of designs, as though it had been around too long to just have one aesthetic.

One of the alcoves off to the right was basically a library. The walls were lined with books and the tables were the same as the others but this time the booths were made of crushed red velvet. Another alcove was all flocked damask wallpaper and material draping from the ceiling with lanterns reminiscent of the kind you'd see at a Turkish bazaar. The booths in that alcove were lower to the ground, just like the tables, and had intricate patterns on the large, overstuffed cushions. Yet another looked more like someone's living room with leather couches and a low coffee table in the middle.

On the side opposite the alcoves was a long bar that was styled like a pub with its own ceiling and everything. Glasses hung from the racks overhead and bottles of all kinds lined the wall. There were more than just a few of each kind of alcohol; there had to be hundreds of bottles there. The glossy black surface of the bar was spotless. I could see that even from here.

The tables in the center of the room were what held my attention the most, though. Dealers and gamblers lined each one. A few of the tables had that distinctive green felt that I'd only ever seen on casino tables before, while others were dark wood and still others were glass.

The vampires we'd been following turned and stared at us. Oh, shit. We looked like a couple of idiots. I sprang away from Beth and straightened my skirt before tossing my hair. "Lead the way, good men," I said in a formal voice that came out completely ridiculous.

But they just nodded and carried on past the tables of people playing cards, toward some booths that were tucked away and dimly lit. I hadn't even been able to see them from the entrance. There were a few other doors and staircases that peeled off from the room, which had been roped off. I glanced up to see rooms above us with glass fronts, the kind of two-way mirror where whoever was in there could see out but we couldn't see in.

That explained why the staircase was so long. We were more like two stories down. It also explained why the bar had its own section of lowered ceiling.

The vampires stopped at one of the roped-off doors and nodded at the guard posted there. He knocked on the door twice, and a few seconds later it opened from the inside.

We went up a short flight of stairs. Vampire one, me, Beth, then vampire two bringing up the rear. My feet were starting to freaking hurt. Sitting against the wall was a vampire that looked like she owned the place. She was watching us like we were ants in her kitchen. Next to her, though, was one of the most intimidating men I'd ever encountered. If I thought she looked like she owned the place it was nothing compared to this guy. And beside him were two young women who looked like they belonged upstairs.

One of our vampire guides turned to face us. "Mr. Atonal owns this club. You will show him respect." There was a viciousness to his voice that left me with the feeling that if we didn't voluntarily we'd be forced to. And he didn't look opposed to violence.

"I thought the leader of the vamps was a woman," I whispered to Beth.

"She is. He just owns the club."

The two women who looked far too young for Mr. Atonal hissed at us. As we approached, I couldn't help but realize how wrong I'd been about the woman who'd sneered at us as we walked in. She definitely didn't look like she owned the club, not when compared to Mr. Atonal.

"I don't *just* own the club," he said in a low voice, easily heard in the quiet VIP room. "I'm the second-in-command to the vampire queen and lord of this domain." He spread his hands pompously.

Oh, fuck. What a dick. "I'm looking for my brother, Henry Foxx."

Atonal squinted. "The human?" He waved his hand dismissively. "He is no concern of mine."

"Hey," I said sharply, causing Atonal to give me a withering glance. "He is a concern of yours because I need to know where he is."

"He got what he deserved. No one cheats in my club," Atonal said and caressed one of the women's thighs, sliding his hand way too high in front of strangers. "You may leave."

Okay, deep breath. Don't back down. "No, I want to know where he is."

"I owe you nothing," the vampire said, his lip curling into an almost-smirk. "I am a powerful vampire, and you are a lowly witch with a few tricks in her bag. This was a one time courtesy. You will leave my club now and never dare to waste my time again."

No. My heart raced. I couldn't leave the club without Henry.

I looked at Beth. She looked back at me, a question in her eyes. Oh no, had she thought I'd run things from here?

I curled my hands into fists. Okay then. My friends had gotten me this far. It looked like I was going to have to put my big girl panties on and handle it from here.

People seemed to fear Karma, so there had to be a reason, right?

I wondered if my powers could be manipulated and

focused, rather than happening when the timing was right. Narrowing my eyes on him, I muttered, "Tiny-dicked jerk." A familiar tingle moved over my skin, and I felt a strange mix of horror and fascination as I held my breath, waiting. Not sure for what.

A second later, Atonal got a strange look on his face like he'd eaten something bad. His muscles jerked. His brows drew together in confusion, and then he gasped and his eyes went wide. Throwing the women off of him, he jumped to his feet, unbuckling his fancy belt faster than I could catch with my eyes before he looked into his pants.

"Turn it back!" he screamed so loud the people beyond the window, even some of the dealers, swung their heads around, looking for who yelled. "Now!"

Beth glanced at me in confusion. I was sure I looked just as shocked as he did. Had I really just...? Could I actually control my powers? And if he realized I'd been the one to do this, what would he do to me?

Especially if I had no idea how to change him back.

But then I saw realization dawn on Beth's face, and rather than looking alarmed, she had the most pleased expression. Here I was trying to figure out whether or not I should be scared. The only thing I could think to do was to follow her lead.

With a snort, Beth pointed at Atonal. "You should be more polite. Emma here is *Karma*."

Atonal gaped at me. His gaze ran from my uncomfortable shoes up to my face. I had no idea what he was thinking, but he still seemed disturbed by whatever *tiny* problem he'd found in his pants.

"I thought Karma was a legend."

I forced a grin and crossed my arms as Beth continued. "The only way to fix it is to *stop* being a tiny-dicked jerk."

Atonal stood staring into his pants for several seconds. "Okay!" he said in a high-pitched, scared voice. "I heard a rumor, but that's all I know!"

Pointing my finger directly at him, as though that was how I controlled the size of his dick, I stepped closer. "What was the rumor? I can make it disappear entirely," I warned.

He yelped and scrambled backward, falling into his chair. "It was rumored that Henry got mixed up with the sirens. That he owes them a blood debt."

Sirens? *Of course* sirens were real too. But was this a bad thing? I glanced at Beth out of the corner of my eye. She looked pale and shaken.

The vampire continued in an emotionless voice. "And we all know that if that's true, it's doubtful he's alive."

Ice moved through my veins, and I felt like his words echoed over and over again through my mind.

"No."

He looked between me and Beth. "I'm guessing Karma isn't familiar with those beasts?"

"He's still alive," I said, and my voice had an angry note.

The vampire's mouth opened, as if he was about to laugh, and then he glanced into his pants and seemed to think better of it. But I didn't care what he said or thought. We'd faced shifters and vampires in my search for my brother, and none of them had managed to hurt Henry. I wasn't about to believe that some fish had.

Beth tugged on the back of my dress. "Let's go."

"No," I said. "Not until he tells us more. Not until he--"

"That's all I know!" The anger in his voice made the two women beside him draw back further.

I glared at him, trying to think of a way karma could hurt him for blaming some sirens on this, and for saying my Henry was probably dead. But my whole body was shaking so hard that my teeth were chattering, and I couldn't think of a way to hurt this man more.

"He's not lying," Beth said, after a tense moment.

"But Henry's still alive," I told her rather than asked.

She hesitated. "There's nothing better we can do for Henry right now than go and follow this lead."

I released a slow breath. Okay, if she believed the vampire, I'd have to have faith that my best friend knew what she was talking about, even if I hated the idea of us leaving this place without Henry. And in the back of my mind, I felt truly afraid for what it meant that my brother was with sirens: creatures that apparently the vampires and witches feared.

Nodding, I turned to go.

"What about fixing my slammer?"

Slammer? Ugh. Some men were just disgusting.

I focused on Atonal and chose my words carefully. "When you've convinced the magic you're not a jerk, that will go away. And be warned, if you try to retaliate and hurt me or kill me or any of my loved ones, it'll disappear entirely and won't come back."

He nodded vigorously with his hand on his crotch. "Understood! You have my word!"

"We gotta go," Beth whispered, more urgently this time.

She grabbed my hand and tugged me all the way down the stairs, through the quiet downstairs, then up the long flight stairs that led back to the club. Lurch watched us in surprise as Beth dragged me toward the main door. I waved as I stumbled behind her, and he grinned.

When we were outside in the relatively cool night air, I yanked back on her arm. "Beth!" I yelled. "Stop."

She listened, stopping right there. Between the parking

lot lights and the moon overhead, I could make out something of her expression. And what I saw scared me.

"What is it?" Goosebumps blossomed on my skin.

"Listen, Emma, the thing is. If he pissed off the sirens, he's not missing. He's dead."

16

DANIEL

Emma and Beth came running through the parking lot like the hounds of hell were on their heels. "Whoa," I yelled, throwing my arms wide as though I could catch them.

Beth managed to skid to a halt, but Emma landed right in my arms. And I'd be lying if I said I didn't like it. Even the bear within me seemed to stand at attention as I got lost in her earthy scent and the soft curves of her body for a moment too long before my gaze snapped down to her and reality came crashing back into me. Why in the world were they running? And why did Emma look so upset?

If those damn vampires gave her any problems, I didn't care how much trouble I caused, I was going to go full bear on them. And even vampires were smart enough to be scared of a bear shifter. Hell, everyone was.

It took Emma a second to recognize me, but as soon as she did, her entire demeanor relaxed and she leaned into me. "My brother's been taken by the sirens!"

I stiffened as my mind started working. "Sirens?" That

could only mean one thing. "They're going to use him in their Ancestral Waters ceremony."

Her eyes went wide. "What does that mean?"

I hesitated, an image of her brother's familiar face popping into my mind. "It means they're going to sacrifice him for a ceremony. It's something the sirens do."

The horror in her expression made my heart ache. "We have to get to him. Now. This second."

If only it was that easy, but the sirens were easily the most powerful group of supernaturals in Mystic Hollow. I'd do everything in my power to save Emma's brother, but this wasn't something we could just run out and do. And I sure as hell wasn't going to take her with me when I faced them. I was willing to risk my life. That wasn't something that came naturally to me, even after I retired, but I wouldn't risk hers.

I shook my head. "No can do. I'm sorry."

She thumped her hand against my chest, her brows drawing together. "What do you mean no can do? Like you're just going to decide to leave my brother to die, and I'm just going to sit here and let it happen?"

"That's not what I--"

She didn't seem to hear me. "Maybe I'm not the same Emma Foxx from back in the day, but I'm not a pushover either. Rick might have thought...no, it doesn't matter what my ex thought, because I'm not that woman. I will save my brother, even if you won't help us."

I felt so many confusing things in that moment. Rick? That was the name of the man she'd married. Apparently, a man who thought she was a pushover. Was he insane? This proud woman was strong and fearless, diving into shifter territory and vampire clubs. But the last thing I wanted was for her to think I was anything like her ex, or that I saw her as anything but the amazing woman that she was.

"I only meant that your brother will be taken care of until their Ancestral Waters ceremony and *then* killed. He's safe until then. And the other good news is that they do that on the mainland. We might not be able to get him wherever they're keeping him right now, but they'll have to come to town to do their ceremony, which means I'll have a chance to rescue him then. Hopefully."

The hand that had thumped my chest seemed to relax. "Okay, as long as you know that sirens or boogie men, I'm getting my brother back."

"I wouldn't expect anything less," I told her, this time unable to hide my smile.

She drew back from me a little, tucking her dark hair behind one ear in an endearing way. "Good. And also, don't think I didn't notice you mentioning you'd be saving him. I'll be right there with you."

I felt my smile widen. Man, it felt like I'd smiled since Emma came back to town than I had in years. But then, she'd always had that effect on me, even when I was just watching her from afar. She had a way of making me enjoy life.

"What now?" Beth asked, and I felt my smile fade away.

Right. I was here for a reason. I couldn't let myself be distracted by a pretty lady.

Pointing toward the door, I nodded. "I was just going in to ask where Henry was."

"Don't bother," Emma said bitterly. "They were no help, other than telling me about the sirens."

"That's a pretty big help." I scratched my jaw. "It's too bad we don't know an alchemist."

Emma gave me a puzzled look, but Beth's eyes lit up. "Oh, my gosh I totally forgot about that."

"What?" Emma asked. "Forgot about what?"

"Alchemists provide the sirens with their offerings to their ancestors. Along with the traditional stuff like fish, shells, anything that honors the ocean and water, they also bring different soaps, purifiers, and other things that are spelled by an alchemist to try and get the waters to flow again."

Emma nodded in understanding. "So, they could get us near the sirens?"

"It's possible, but at the very least I could try to get the information from one," I said.

Beth snorted. "No. You will not. I know you're all shifty and all that, but you're not a witch. If anyone stands a chance at getting that info, it's me."

She checked her watch. "We have to go back in there, and you two have to act like you're not with me, because the alchemist I know is in there, selling potions to idiotic young witches who think they're buying love potions, when they're really buying lust potion."

"I think we should take more of an official route," I said. "And that you two should let me handle this." None of this sat right with me. They were putting themselves in danger and it made my protective instincts that much harder to control.

When Beth turned to go back into the club, and Emma followed, I realized I didn't have a choice. Ever since Beth had opened her business years ago, she'd found a way to involve herself in a lot of supernatural cases. Most of them involved small things: missing items, cheaters, discovering hexers, removing curses, etc. I never minded, because she had a way of getting to the bottom of things and leaving everyone involved feeling like they'd won, which was a hard thing to do as a police officer sometimes. But as I slowly followed behind the two of them, I felt in my gut that a missing brother and trouble with sirens was more than they should be involved in.

But knowing it and getting them to listen to me were two different things.

I sighed and hurried to catch up with them. If they were going to do this anyway, I could at least keep an eye on them.

The bouncer at the front door did a double take when he saw Beth coming. His eyes widened as he jumped out of the way and opened the door as fast as he could move. Beth looked over her shoulder. "You two can wait out here."

Emma and I exchanged a fast look. I had zero intention of letting Beth go in there alone, and wished they hadn't gone in without me before, too. Hurrying forward, I tried to go in after her, but the bouncer stepped in the way.

Emma sighed beside me. "Let us in."

The vampire chuckled. "You don't have the power your friend does."

"No," Emma said in an even tone. "I have my own." She narrowed her eyes as I watched in amazement.

The vampire may as well have turned to stone for all the emotion he showed as he said, "You're not allowed back in. Antonal's orders. And old ass men aren't allowed in either."

"*Old*?" For some reason, I loved the outrage in her face as she glanced from the bouncer to me. It was like in her eyes I was some kind of young stud.

I turned and looked at some of the twenty-something-year-olds in line, trying to hide the blush that was no doubt staining my cheeks. "It's okay--"

"It's not okay! What in the world is with all these people using the word old like it's an insult?" She looked from me to the bouncer. "Age isn't something to be ashamed of! And I'll tell you, I'd rather have a nice-looking man with a face like his then some young guy who doesn't even know how to drive a car properly."

Drive a *car*? Was she talking about...? I felt my cheeks get even hotter.

"And another thing: I think you'll find that I am allowed into the club, as is my friend," Emma said, her voice rising. She narrowed her eyes as I watched in amazement. "Your job brings a bit too much power," she said as she tossed her hair. "I think you're getting a little big for your britches."

The vampire furrowed his brows. "Okay?" But then he blinked. A second later he looked down at himself, his fingers trying to grab on to his belt as what had started out as regular jeans turned into skinny jeans, at least in terms of their size. Suddenly it was very obvious that the bouncer had been skipping leg day, and the jeans tightened even more until I had to avert my eyes. The last thing I wanted to see was the outline of this guy's junk, and that's where it was heading.

"Go," he shouted. "I'm sorry! Make it stop!"

Emma cocked her head. "Stop acting so cocky and your pants will loosen. When you're not too big for them."

He nodded vigorously and tried to unbutton his jeans as we walked past.

Beth stood inside the door and turned to us. "I told you, you can't be with me. I need to do this alone. Dance floor," she yelled. "It's the only way this works!" She pushed at Emma's shoulders so she'd follow me out onto the dance floor. "Go!"

I shrugged and held out my hand. Emma gave me a small smile and the next thing I knew, we were slow dancing to a very fast song. I wished I could say that I was more aware of our surroundings, but in that moment, with Emma looking up at me as we swayed back and forth, I wasn't. Hell,

I wasn't even aware of the other sweaty bodies gyrating on the dance floor even though I'd seen them only a moment ago.

"So, what happened with the vampires?" I asked. I had to pull her close and bend forward with my ear to her lips to listen. It broke the moment though, which was what I needed. I couldn't afford to be so distracted.

"Long story short, I used my unique abilities to convince the owner of this place to give us some info, which was that Henry pissed off the sirens. That was all he knew."

"Well, it gets us started, anyway." As we swung on the dance floor, I kept my eyes open for Beth, and off of Emma. Beth floated around the room, apparently looking for her target.

All the bodies that I had been oblivious to before were now all too present. Everywhere I looked, the place was filled with college aged kids that were theoretically doing something akin to dancing. The way some of the women were shaking their behinds and grinding them into their dance partner's crotch was enough to make me feel ancient. When had dancing become little more than sex with clothes on? The bouncer was right, I was an old ass man.

I pulled my thoughts back to the situation at hand. "I won't stop looking for your brother," I said. "We have a good lead, but that won't stop me following up on others."

Her dark brows drew together, twin arches over those deep brown eyes of hers. For a second, I couldn't look away. There were so many songs about blue-eyed girls, but tonight was the first time I wished I could sing, just so I could talk about her eyes.

Man, this woman had done a number on me. She was turning me into some cheesy idiot.

"Why are you helping me?" Emma finally asked. There

was a mix of surprise and relief in her eyes. Had she really thought that I'd hear that sirens were involved and run off? When the surprise wore off, I could also see a healthy dose of skepticism in there as well.

"I understand loss." I watched the idiot kids dancing and probably taking ridiculous amounts of drugs around me and sighed. I hated telling this story. I pushed the emotions down so I could relay what happened without getting over-whelmed. "My wife and best friend were on their way to Shawsville to pick up a birthday present for me when they were in a freak accident. A fuel truck crashed into them and exploded." I chuckled humorlessly. "Those things are really hard to blow up, though you wouldn't think so. But it did, killing them both. It also started a fire. It was a dry and windy summer, so it turned into a wildfire. The worst one our region has ever seen, as a matter of fact."

I wanted to say more. I wanted to pull that moment together with this moment when she was scared for her brother, but I couldn't seem to form the words. Because everyone knew that Emma had lost so much over the years already. It seemed like the right thing to tell her I under-stood, but the wrong thing to compare any of our losses as if they were the same. Loss was always different. That was something I'd learned in my professional life and my personal life.

Emma's gaze was filled with so much empathy that I wished I could curl around her. Instead, I continued holding her gently, diving into those eyes of hers. At last, her sweet voice came. "I'm so sorry. That had to have been awful." We both fell quiet for a moment before she spoke again. "I, uh. I'm going through a messy divorce. I've tried to keep it from Travis, my son, but he's picking up on more of it than I would like. Smart ass kid." She rolled her eyes and fixed her stare on me. "Rick, my husband, cheated. Bad. It was awful, left me pretty much a total wreck. It may or may not have had something to do with me coming back to Mystic Hollow."

My blood boiled. How dare this Rick guy treat her like that? Emma was sweet, kind, and joyful, and for someone to stomp all over that made me want to show them exactly what my bear thought of the situation. My bear paced within me, eager to be released so he could wreak some havoc. I could hardly suppress the growl that wanted to vibrate out of me as it was. "I'm sorry he did that to you. If you'd like, I can kill him and make it look like a bear attack," I offered.

She burst out laughing. I spun her and lowered her into a dip. As she arched her back and let herself relax, I heard a ripping sound. Emma gasped and her eyes widened. "Oh, no," she whispered, one hand suddenly clutching her stomach.

"What was that?" I pulled her close again, gently taking her hand that had been resting on her stomach and putting it around my waist as we began to sway again.

Her cheeks reddened. I could tell even in the low light, which meant they were probably actually flaming red in the right lighting. "My girdle."

It took all I had not to burst out laughing. She would probably think I was laughing at her though, which I wasn't, just the situation. "Emma, you don't need that. There's nothing wrong with curves." Hell, I'd thought she looked a little stiff. "Relax. Really, I—"

"Sir?" A voice behind me cut me off suddenly. Emma jerked away and looked at the guy behind me with wide eyes.

Turning slowly, I faced one of the vampires I knew guarded the door to the VIP section downstairs. "Yes?"

"The boss would like a word," he said.

After nodding at the stooge, I gave Emma a small bow. "Next time," I said, then followed the crony toward the downstairs door.

Time to do my job.

17

"**T**his has been the longest three days of my life," I said with a long moan as I pushed the book away. We'd been researching nonstop, but there was *not* much info to be found about sirens. All we knew for sure was what Beth had gotten from her contact. They came inland to the beach to do their ceremony every full moon near the waterfall. The internet said the sirens lived in massive mansions on tiny unplottable islands off the mainland. They also had a flotilla of sorts, but that was spoken about even less in the books.

"So, we're going to do this," I muttered. "We are." I took another bite of the brownie Deva brought for courage. The rich, chocolaty square practically melted on my tongue. It was so gooey and delicious. "Why can't we see their tiny islands?" I asked.

"Because their magic prevents it." Beth took another brownie, too. "It's like impenetrable fog."

"This is our only chance." Deva set out a plate of cookies now that the brownies were demolished, the scent of the warm chocolate chips and macadamia nuts making my stomach growl quietly even though it was full of brownie and should be satisfied with that. "But they are *mean*, Emma. This could go very wrong. They might even kill Henry as soon as they see us. They're unpredictable at best and their moods seem to shift as quickly as waves coming in to the shore from what I've heard."

"But you're sure Henry should be safe until then?" I asked, my pulse picking up.

"Yes. They need a living sacrifice for this to work," Beth said, and there was only a small note in her voice that reminded me I'd asked the question a thousand times already.

"And we still don't have any idea why they grabbed Henry out of everyone and if this had anything to do with his gambling?"

Deva sighed. "We've all been following up with every contact we have, and no one has a clue."

Still. I swore with their phones always going off, I constantly felt a strange kind of hope that one of their texts or calls would be with valuable information to make any of this make sense. Unfortunately, so far it'd been a bunch of supernaturals who didn't have a clue about Henry's disappearance.

I grabbed a cookie, deciding it was better to focus on the food than my waning hope. Was I comfort eating? Maybe. Not that my friends were judging. "Why are you doing this to me? Sweets are my weakness."

Murmurs of agreement came from the other women around mouthfuls of cookies. We were all at our wits end when it came to research and, personally, I was getting impatient for the full moon, when this weird ceremony was supposed to take place. I just wanted Henry back safe and sound.

A man walked by the storefront and dropped his gum wrapper right on the sidewalk in front of us. He couldn't see us because of the tint on her glass, but we could see him fine. He hadn't accidentally dropped it either. It wasn't like it fell out of his pocket as he was trying to tuck it away. No. He barely even crumpled it up before he dropped it.

"Asshole," Buster said with a growl and a flick of his tail.

I'd been practicing my magic every moment we weren't researching. This wasn't the first moment I'd encountered like this, but it still gave me a thrill to intentionally use my magic. I waved my hand and the man stopped and bent over, coughing hard. A few seconds later, he coughed up a gum wrapper. He turned back in our direction to stare down at the wrapper he'd thrown on the ground.

Looking around in panic, he rushed forward and picked up his discarded wrapper and stuffed both in his pocket. He practically ran away after that. I vaguely remembered hearing about weird stuff happening when I lived here as a kid, but I'd always chalked it up to adults being paranoid or not smart enough to realize what was actually going on. I was such a brat. All the arrogance and invincibility of a typical teenager.

"Hmph." I nodded. Served him right.

"Nice," Buster said, then stretched in his patch of warm sunshine. The sun highlighted that he wasn't just a black cat but a tabby cat. The warm light made the dark brown stripes stand out against the rest of his black fur.

Everyone laughed at the horrified expression on the guy's face before we all turned back to our respective books and kept reading. The books my girls had produced were more than just a little old; they were ancient, and as such, were treated with care, so when I dropped cookie crumbs on the page I hurriedly swiped them off, hoping they didn't leave any chocolate or residue behind. The last thing I wanted was to piss off any of the witches that had loaned us the books. My girls had scoured their homes and the home libraries of all their witchy friends, hoping we'd find something more helpful in these books. I knew a little chocolate smudge wouldn't piss off my friends, but the others? I had no idea about them.

"Oh, no." Deva slapped her hand on the table, her voice a groan, like she'd just remembered a dentist appointment or something.

I looked up to see her staring out the windows with her eyes wide before narrowing into a furrowed glare. Then the front doorbell jingled.

We all swung our gazes around to see Deva's ex walk in the door with his arms full of African violets. There must have been over a hundred of the tiny purple flowers. "He keeps doing this," she whispered. "These are my favorite. Seems like ever since we broke up, he's suddenly remembering my preferences. He didn't give a crap when we were together though."

The women and animals stared coldly at Harry as he set the violets on the table and backed away, making tiny bows and with his eyes glued to Deva. "I know I don't deserve a second chance, but I won't stop trying. I love you, Deva. Name the price and I'll pay it."

He briefly scanned his eyes over everyone else, saluting the rest of us before he backed out the door.

"That boy didn't know what he had until it was gone," Carol tutted as she shook her head sadly and grabbed another cookie. "Those are pretty, though."

"They're toxic to animals," Buster murmured from the floor. "Burn them."

"How about you just don't eat them," Beth countered. "Problem solved."

"*Human,*" Buster muttered, then huffed and rolled around in his sunbeam until he was the shape of a kidney bean with all four paws in the air. I'd seen cats in that position before and it was always a trap. They put their fluffy bellies on display, making you want to pet them, but then as soon as you did the paws and claws and teeth captured your hand. I wasn't sure if he was like every other cat I knew, but I wasn't about to test that theory and fall for the trap. "I think I'll poop in your shoe later," he purred with satisfaction.

I was surprised it wasn't Marble, the tortoiseshell cat, that was giving Beth a hard time, but she was off sleeping in the corner. Buster and Beth had an odd love-hate relationship, as I imagined many owners did with their cats.

"Hey," I interrupted their argument. We'd been hanging out at Beth's office for three days and all they'd done is go back and forth. It was their dynamic. And it was getting old. "Can we focus?"

"Right," Carol said before turning to look at Deva. "You're going to fall back into old patterns if you get back with him."

"He's trying really hard, but I don't think I could ever love him again." Deva delicately stroked one of the flower's petals before dropping to the fuzzy leaf that lay underneath. "But I'm going to enjoy these flowers, though. They *are* my favorite, after all." Her tone made me wonder if she would actually hold out against Harry's attempts at romancing his way back into her heart. When she arched an eyebrow and stared off into space, a memory probably replaying itself in her mind, I saw the resolve settle on her like a cloak. "I will *not*, however, make another damn sandwich for any man!"

"Yeah!" I yelled. "Except, you know. At your restaurant."

"Or if it's your turn to cook. Cause that's fair," Carol said with a shrug.

"But we get the sentiment and totally agree!" Beth chimed in with her fist in the air. "Girl power!"

"So, how about a different guy? You might want to make the *right* guy a sandwich, or maybe he'll want to make all the sandwiches. You'll be showered in sandwiches and love," I said, my mind wandering off to what I was starting to think the rest of my life might be like without Rick hanging over my head like the sword of Damocles, although that implied I had power over the situation, which hadn't been true, at least not until recently. It was more like he was the axe the executioner was getting ready to swing. I was just waiting for the blow to land. Sure, the initial blow had been finding out about the cheating, but until the divorce was settled and I knew where I stood, it felt like there was the possibility of another blow that could be even worse than the first just around the corner.

Buster lifted his head blinking his jade green eyes slowly. "You can make me a sandwich. Tuna, hold the mayo."

"Shut up!" We all yelled in unison. He sniffed and rolled over, giving us his back.

Deva blushed. "I can't even consider a different guy, or any guy really, until I've healed myself."

Daniel's face flashed through my mind, followed quickly by Rick's. Ugh. "I need the same thing. Time. The heart will heal, though. At least that's what I keep telling myself."

Everyone nodded, but I couldn't help but hope that Daniel would still be single once I was ready. I also hoped that the sirens would be reasonable, that we wouldn't have to fight them for Henry, and that I'd get him back unharmed, or at the very least alive.

That was a whole lot of hope floating around.

18

EMMA

Sighing, I let my head fall back against the headrest. Beth and I were waiting for Deva and Carol to come out of Carol's house. Deva had some stuff she'd baked that she hoped would help us on our mission. I was agitated though, antsy to get to the place the sirens were going to be arriving for their ceremony and get Henry out of trouble. A good chunk of me wanted to yell at them to hurry up, but that was just me being impatient, so I took another breath and slowly released it.

"Mystic Hollow moves a little slower than the rest of the world," Beth mused beside me. She was putting on a bright shade of pink lipstick in the rearview mirror and fluffing her mass of wavy blonde hair. She was wearing a pink low-cut top and jeans.

"I forgot." And I had. So much had changed, but certainly the slow pace of the place hadn't.

"But that should be fun with your next relationship."

I stiffened. Huh?

She winked. "You know, the men around here like to take their *time*."

I felt my cheeks turn beat red. "I am in *no* way thinking about relationships, men, dating, or anything of that sort!"

She laughed, crinkles forming at the corners of her blue eyes. "Really? Because I saw the way you two were dancing. And it looked more than a little friendly."

Was I so obvious? My heart raced. "Not even a little."

"Really?" She arched a brow.

"*Really.*"

"Because he has the most stunning blue eyes I've ever seen."

"He has green eyes." I stopped myself too late.

Her grin widened.

"Shut up," I mumbled and looked away from her.

Daniel was cute, but I wasn't twenty and running after a hot guy with my mouth hanging open. I had my brother to find, my life to get in order, and my powers to figure out. Plus, I swore this was already the longest darn day of my life. There was definitely no energy left for thinking about the handsome shifter.

A shifter I had learned a lot about the last few days. Apparently, shifters weren't like werewolves. They could control when they changed, and most of them changed into wolves rather than anything crazy mythical. Daniel was unique, they'd explained, because he was a bear shifter. A bear?

I still hadn't quite wrapped my mind around it all.

My gaze moved back to the house, and I tried not to tap my thigh. I was exhausted, but couldn't help but stare at the little house with the porch swing and colorful, wild-looking flowers planted around the yard. The place screamed *Carol*, from the dozens of windchimes hanging on the porch to the suncatchers reflecting in the windows. But Deva had been living with her for over a year, and there were little touches of her too. A couple of potted plants, all in a row. A stone walking path that looked new and carefully tended. I had heard she'd even started a garden in the back.

It was strange, them living together. Carol was wild and fun, but definitely liked her space. For some reason, the fact that she'd never married, or even seemed mildly interested in dating, had seemed normal for her.

But organized Deva living with Carol? I never thought it would happen. Unlike my marriage, Deva and her husband started out so perfect. High school sweethearts. A sweet proposal. Everything that people say should lead to living happily-ever-after. She'd settled into being married and having kids like it was what she was always meant for. And now, picturing her single and living in the chaos that was Carol's home? It was hard to imagine. But maybe good for both of them.

"How are they as roommates?"

Beth grinned next to me, flashing those dimples of hers. "Surprisingly, they're doing great. Deva likes feeling like she has someone to take care of still, with her girls scattered around the world and her ex gone. She was getting lonely in her big house. And Carol has always seemed so happy to live alone, but I swear she's been giddy since Deva moved in. You know she thrives with an audience."

"She says that about you," I said, giving a tired smile.

Beth rolled her eyes and tugged at her long blonde hair, something she'd been doing since we were kids. "I'm glad for them. But I honestly give it another year before Deva starts dating Marquis."

"Really?" I lifted my head from the headrest, suddenly intrigued. I'd thought she was more likely to get back with her ex than some new guy. "Tell me all about the mysterious Marquis."

"You know him. Remember? He was short, big glasses, and braces. Sweet, but really quiet."

"*That* Marquis?" I was shocked. I tried to match him up with the confident Deva and couldn't.

"Well, he got taller in high school. In college, he lost his braces and filled out a bit. Now, he's a handsome guy, and the town doctor. He's still kind of a shy guy, but there's no question he's got a thing for her. I think he's just waiting for any sign she might be ready."

I leaned back and closed my eyes. "I'd love to see her with someone like that. He sounds like the opposite of Harry."

"He is." She sighed. "But Deva doesn't even seem to be willing to acknowledge him."

"Give her time," I said.

Time. That was what I needed too. I might have been thrown into a new life, but in so many ways I was still the same me. Deva and I were similar in that way. We wanted to move on, but we weren't there quite yet.

"Shit," Beth whispered. "Why does he have to be here, now?"

My eyes flashed open and I glanced at my friend. She looked like she'd seen a ghost. Her face was white as a sheet. When I looked past her, I could see a man and woman walking toward us on the sidewalk. "Who is it?" I said in a low voice. Both of our windows were down. I didn't want him to hear me.

"My ex," she hissed without ever moving her eyes from where they were fixed ahead of her, not looking at her ex and his new woman or at me, just focused on trying to ignore the whole situation. "He left me for *her*."

It hit me. That was Roger? I'd seen pictures, yeah, but the guy had aged more than I imagined. I tried to picture

him from their vacation photos over the years, and guessed I
could see the resemblance.

"Beth?" The man, admittedly handsome if one liked a
dad-bod, bent over and peered into the car. His blue eyes
twinkled as though he found something altogether too
funny, and he flashed a car salesman smile at her. "Is that
you?"

"Yeah." Beth's hands fluttered in her lap. "It's me." Her
voice was high but quiet, as though she was struggling to get
the words out as she stared down at her hands without ever
making eye contact with him.

I leaned over, making sure to give him my best unim-
pressed look, and peered up at the woman. The *other*
woman.

Holy shit. She looked like a younger version of Beth,
which was insulting in more ways than I could count.

"Of all the bullshit!" I hissed.

No. Absolutely not.

Throwing open my car door, I lurched out of the car and
slammed it shut. Fury burned through my veins like lava.
"You've got a lot of nerve, asshole!"

Her ex, Roger, straightened from where he'd still been
leaning over Beth and looked at me all startled and hoity-
toity. "Excuse me. Who the hell are you?"

A pang of guilt swept through me that we'd never really
met. Sure, I'd seen photos, but they'd gotten together shortly
after Deva's wedding twenty years ago, so I hadn't met him
when I'd come into town for the event. And Rick hadn't
wanted to go back after that, so we hadn't. Something I
regretted with every fiber of my being. He'd controlled so
much of my life without me even realizing it. I wasn't going
to let this jerkwad make Beth feel bad about herself the way
Rick did to me.

I stalked around the hood of the car until I was less than a couple feet from the two of them. "You heard me. You don't get to speak to her! You cheated, with this..." I waved my hands at the other woman. "Creepy version of Beth. Baby version of Beth. Is that the problem? You wanted Beth but you like 'em young?"

His face turned dark red and a fury that made me think he may be hiding an even darker side passed through his eyes. "Now hold on—"

"No, *you* hold on! Karma is going to get you. And you!" I pointed first at her ex then at the woman, girl, whatever. "I'd bet money you knew he was in a long-term, committed relationship, with a woman he'd been promising to marry for almost twenty years, when you started fooling around, didn't you? Didn't you? But you didn't give a crap about his *partner* and how she felt. You just wanted to get yours. Well, I've got news for you little girl: he's going to dump you faster than a hot potato when he gets bored. Look forward to that."

"No, he's not, because I'm the woman he always needed. And I don't look like her," the woman suddenly sneered, as if the dummy had just now realized we were talking about her.

But she really did. "Yeah, you do. The same hair, the same eyes. Holy crap. Tiffany?"

Hell. Beth's parents had accidentally gotten pregnant again when Beth was seventeen. Tiffany had been a toddler when I'd left. But there was no way. *No way* her sister could actually...

She tilted her head up, and I realized that she had a pig-shaped nose that she'd tried to sculpt with a pound of makeup to look more like Beth's. "Yeah? So what?"

It felt like the floor dropped out from under me. I knew he'd been cheating on her with someone younger, but why hadn't Beth told me? I knew the answer immediately. Because it would've killed her to even say the words aloud. Husbands cheating happened all too often, but leaving their wife for her younger sister? Disgusting.

"Beth practically raised you," I said in disbelief.

It was one of the reasons Beth had decided to go to the local community college for her business degree instead of away with me. But then she'd had to drop out after her associate's degree, because her parents started having serious health issues and needed her to help. Sometimes when we talked late at night, she'd sound so wistful when I talked about college. I'd try to change the topic, but she said she loved to live through me, since we'd both been business majors.

"I didn't need her to raise me," the woman said, tossing her blonde hair.

"Yeah, you did." A cold feeling rushed through me. "And it's heartbreaking that you could do this to her. But I want you to know something: Beth doesn't need you, because we're her family now."

I was shaking, and that cold feeling inside of me kept growing. A person needed to have a frozen heart to steal a man from her own sister. Not that he was some prize to steal. But if Tiffany wasn't a trash human being, she would've helped Beth realize that Roger was a bad guy, rather than take him for herself.

"You--" I struggled for the words to express just how angry I was at them.

"Emma," Beth interrupted in an amused voice as she got out of the car. Her door slammed shut behind her as she came up to me and quietly said, "You're glowing."

I looked down at myself to find I was, indeed, glowing.

Like a lightning bug. My skin was luminous and not in the way all those night eye creams talked about either.

When I glanced back up, Beth's ex and his child-girl-friend were hurrying down the street, him with his arm around her protectively. "She needs your protection because she's done one of the worst things a woman can do to another woman!" I screamed after them.

Beth blew out a laugh, bending over at the waist and hee-hawing a deep gut laugh. At one point, I swear she squeaked like a bike horn. "Emma," she wheezed. "That was amazing! What did you do to them?"

With the strangest certainty, I said, "I'm not sure exactly. Sometimes Karma takes a bit of time, but it'll be good, no matter what it is. Or bad if you're them, I guess."

"Good," Beth said, and there was a sad note to her voice.

"I'm so sorry," I said, fighting the urge to pull her into a hug.

"Surprisingly, it's getting easier."

"But you raised her, you--"

"I never did any of that thinking that she'd owe me, or even that she'd appreciate me. I took care of her because it was the right thing to do."

That was the first time I felt my powers race over my skin, sending every hair standing on end. It seemed that every time I used my abilities, it felt different. "Well, you did something good, and the universe knows that."

She smirked at me. "I guess I'll trust that karma knows what it's doing, or should I say she."

I nodded, feeling strange. A breeze rolled over me, and I swore my powers scattered away from me like leaves in the wind. I even stared into the sky, expecting to see something. But the dark sky was the same.

Karma, I realized, wasn't just popping tires. It took time.

It worked in mysterious ways. But I had no doubt Tiffany and the ex would feel the bite of my powers, and that Beth would be rewarded for being a good person.

Having powers was definitely starting to have its perks.

"I'm going to go give those two a little present."

I jerked at the high-pitched voice, searching for the source of the sound. What I found was a crow on a branch staring at us

Beth said, "We shouldn't.."

"*You* shouldn't. Humans pooping on humans is strange."

The bird lifted off the branch and about a dozen more left the tree, heading for her ex and her sister. At first I just stared in confusion, but around the corner, I heard a chorus of screaming and swearing, and then it hit me.

I looked at Beth. Beth looked at me. And then we both started laughing like idiots. Being a witch, or whatever, definitely had its perks.

A minute later, I heard the sound of a door being thrown open. Carol came out of the house first, lugging a big duffel bag behind her. Deva wasn't far behind her with her arms full of bags as well. It looked like we were vacationing for a week. But this was my first supernatural adventure, so I wasn't about to second-guess the things they thought we needed.

We all piled into the car, and Carol started handing out small burlap bags. "Hex bags," she explained.

"Aren't those dangerous to keep in the house?" I asked.

Carol giggled as she untied the long string on one. "Here, put it under your shirt; wear the hex bag like a necklace. And they aren't dangerous, not if you're an experienced witch and don't make careless mistakes."

"Oh, I feel silly." I laughed and tied the leather string around my neck. "What does this do?"

"If you yank it hard enough, it will tear away from the leather. Then you throw them at someone's feet and it'll temporarily incapacitate them." Carol handed Beth one as she started to pull away from the curb, then stopped and pulled her phone out of her pocket instead.

I glanced over to see her son's name on the screen.

"Oh," Beth said with pleasure. "It's the twins. They're at St. Bartholomew's college."

I knew how much of an unexpected joy it was to get a phone call from your teenager who was away at school. And also how it made that little ball of worry form in your stomach until you answered and knew they were okay.

She hit the speaker button. "Hey, cupcake!"

"Hey, Mom. What are you up to?" The deep voice of her son rang out over the speaker.

"Nothing, sweetie. Just hanging out with my girls." Beth shrugged as Carol handed Deva a sharpened wooden stake out of her bag and then, after a moment's debate, handed Deva and me a small blade each. "How are you and your sister?"

"I'm here too," a young woman's bubbly voice said, which must be Ava. "Are you having book club?"

Deva and I hid our snickers behind our hands while Beth silently laughed and Carol slapped her thigh in amusement.

"Yep," Beth said. "Book club."

"Well, we just wanted to check in," Noah said. "I hope you enjoy your boring Saturday night. Try not to get too crazy with all those books and wine."

We all chuckled.

"I happen to like my books, thank you very much," Beth said in a teasing voice. "Anyway, we're about to start. Do you need anything before I go?

"Nope, just wanted to say hi!" Ava sounded just like her mom and it warmed my heart to think that somewhere out in the world there were two people who had the same goodness and strength in them that Beth did. I wondered if they had any abilities. I'd have to ask Beth the next time we had a chance to talk.

"Goodnight, sweeties. Be safe. Love you!" Beth tapped on the red end call button. For a moment after she hung up, she just looked at her phone, and I wondered if she was thinking about what had just happened with her ex and what her kids would think of it.

I knew I had the same reaction to a lot of the encounters I'd had with Rick since we split up. Eventually she just smiled and shook her head before putting the car in drive and pulling away.

"Boring. I wish. They really think anyone older than them just curls up around a fire, don't they?" she asked with a laugh lacing her voice, sounding more like herself than when her ex had stopped by earlier. I wasn't sure why it bothered me so much, but I was sure that one of the things I had come back to Mystic Hollow for was to help my friends, and for Beth that seemed to be helping her see her self-worth again, and give her the ability to give her ex the middle finger if she wanted to. I wished someone had done the same for me and Rick, but if wishes were fishes and all that.

"My son is the same way," I said. "Travis seems to think I'm best at laundry and cooking dinner for him when he's home from college and not much else. At least not right now. I'm sure that will change as he gets older. At least I hope so."

"Eat this." Deva handed us each a sugar cookie, which was a good distraction before my thoughts turned melancholy. "It should make any powers you already have even stronger."

I bit into the treat and moaned. "How do you do this? I've baked a million cookies for school bake sales and none of mine ever turned out like this. You're a goddess in the kitchen, I swear."

Deva beamed, her smile so wide she got dimples. "Every time you eat something I cook, it's the best compliment ever."

"Oh, here, I almost forgot." Carol pulled out a baggie of ear plugs from the duffel. "These are the kind that they use for the shooting range. It'll keep us from being swayed by the sirens' songs."

We all put them in, and the only person that it was at all noticeable on was Deva because of her very short hair.

"You better hang between us to try to keep them hidden," I suggested.

"Or don't put them in until needed," Beth suggested with a shrug as she glanced in the rearview mirror at our friend.

Deva nodded her head. "They're uncomfortable, anyway. I'll put them in at the first sign of trouble."

"That's it, then," Carol said. "Deva's got another cookie for protection and I've got some necklaces for protection as well, but other than that, we're ready. Probably best to eat the protection cookie when we get there. Same for putting the necklaces on. I want to make sure that we're all covered for as long as possible."

I turned and nodded at Carol, agreeing with her before turning to face forward once more. "Let's go get my brother."

19

EMMA

As we turned off the main road, the trees on both sides of us seemed to crowd the tiny road to the point that I worried we might hit low hanging branches as we drove. When the road circled closer to the ocean, there were breaks in the trees to the rocky cliffs beyond. They were oddly illuminated by the final rays of the setting sun.

Vaguely, I remembered what little I knew of this lake and the waterfall. It was said to be one of the most beautiful places in town. But even as a kid, my parents had warned me about going on these lands. It was private property, and trespassers were dealt with.

But as we continued on, the trees parted as we approached a parking lot. Ahead of us was a massive cliff, without the smallest trace of a waterfall or lake. I frowned, scanning the area, but found nothing of the beautiful place I'd heard described so many times.

"I thought it was a waterfall," I whispered. We parked at the edge of the sand, in an empty, beat-up parking lot that desperately needed repaving. The concrete had turned gravelly, to the point that it was past saving and the whole thing would need to be dug up and redone.

The area the parking lot sat on was raised, almost like it was at the top of a little hill with the cliff face to one side and the ocean to the other, and the path down to the beach area was a steady downward slope between them.

There was a sad note to Deva's voice as she said, "It's been dry for years. But this is where they do their ritual on the full moon, where the river used to fall into the sea. You can't really see it from here, but just around that bend," Deva pointed to where the coastline curved slightly out of sight, "the beach ends and there's a rocky area that used to be a pool for the waterfall before it met the ocean."

The four of us got out of the car and shuffled toward the edge of the parking lot until we could see the water below and the spot that Deva had talked about. I glanced between the area that looked like where the waterfall had come from and where it would have pooled before meeting the ocean.

As I looked down the path, I saw several sirens already lined the rocky shore, even though it wasn't fully dark yet. Even as I watched, the sunset seemed to fade until grey light was all that was left. But even beneath that light, I could see that the women were gorgeous. Like trophy wives with fish tails. Their hair was long and wild, yet somehow looked like perfection. I could swear it glinted in the remaining light like gold and silver. Honestly, it reminded me a little of fish scales, which made sense.

"If they start singing and it gets through our ear plugs, we'll do anything they ask," Carol whispered, a healthy dose of both fear and awe in her voice. "*Anything*."

"Hang on a second," I said quietly, pulling out one of the plugs. "How am I hearing you guys fine, but these are supposed to somehow be effective?"

"I spelled them." Carol grinned at me, clearly proud of herself. "They will only really block out the power of the siren songs, but not talking. We might even hear a little of the songs, but not be enchanted by them. I'm not quite sure about that part of it, but it should work. Neat, huh?"

"Wow. Yeah. That seems like it would be an advanced spell," I said, trying to acknowledge what I thought was probably some hard work, but not wanting to sound patronizing or as though I didn't appreciate it. Praising my friends felt a little like a double edged sword these days since I wasn't sure what was considered easy and what was hard for them to do. Yet another thing to add to my ever expanding list of things to chat with them about when we had time.

Carol beamed at me. "It was! It took me most of the day to get it down. I'm about ninety-nine percent sure it'll work."

Well, couldn't ask for better than the same percentage they used for contraception. Plus, it was better than no percent. I scarfed the last of my protection cookie and pretended it was a courage cookie as well as I said, "Let's go."

We walked down the winding path. It took a while, but it was the only really safe way to get down to the shore below without risking a broken ankle. Even the path, which was supposed to be safe, was a lot of sandy dirt and rocks with some planks of wood in it to make steps. Occasionally, when there was a particularly steep area, there would be a section of handrail as well, though it was wood of course, and since it was wood it was warped and split. Just looking at it gave me splinters, so I kept my hands to myself and focused on where I was putting my feet. I tried to avoid the rocky areas, hoping to make our descent as quiet as possible.

As soon as we got close, we were met at the end of the path by two men. It wasn't until we got really close that I realized they were sirens as well. Their features were a little alien. A little too sharp to be human. They had high, angular cheekbones and noses that looked a little flat. They almost reminded me of a snake. Their skin was pearlescent. It didn't matter the shade; all of them had a sheen to them that made them seem even more fish-like. When one of the men tilted his head and looked at us, his eyes blinked, but not in the way I expected. A clear third eyelid, like a snake's, flicked over the surface. My guess was that it was so they could protect their eyes while underwater but still see. That didn't mean it didn't creep me out, though. I had to pull my gaze down to compose myself, only to realize that it was the worst thing I could have done. Were they naked?

I swallowed hard and raised my head, willing myself not to blush as I looked past the two men that stood silently in front of us. "We're looking for my brother," I said loudly. "Henry Foxx."

All the gathered women that had been lounging at the edge of the ocean jerked their heads toward us when I said my brother's name. One of them hissed in our direction while another of them separated from the group, and as she stood, her fins sort of smoked. Her long, silvery-platinum hair seemed to dry almost instantly and form beautiful natural waves that most women, including myself, would envy. By the time she was fully out of the water, she had legs. Long, perfectly smooth legs that if given some heels would have men falling to the ground and weeping.

As my gaze took her in I was thankful that her long hair covered her boobs since she wasn't wearing a shirt, just like the two men who were still blocking our path. At least she had on a loin cloth of a sort though. As she got closer, her eyes glittered like sapphires in the light, but there was something cold and harsh in them, something that made me want to run in the opposite direction, but I couldn't. Not when I was so close to getting Henry back. Several more of the sirens followed her, all similarly dressed with the loin cloth motif being the main, or rather, only, item of clothing they wore.

"These are our sacred grounds," she said in a deep, formal voice. "You must leave at once."

"I want my brother back. Where's Henry?" I demanded.

She let out a little screech at his name but her voice was drowned out by the sound of an approaching boat. We all turned toward the coast to see a small speed boat coming closer to shore. Behind it, the moon was peeking over the horizon, washing everything in a pale light, including the rapidly approaching boat. Even though it was still bobbing over the waves as it came closer and closer to the shoreline, I could see that there was a man tied up in the center area. He had some sort of bag over his head. My heart raced with anxiety.

It was Henry. It had to be.

For an overwhelming second, I just wanted to start running. I didn't care about supernaturals, magic, or sirens; I just wanted to hold my brother and know that he was okay.

Unless someone else had pissed the sirens off enough to warrant being tied up and blindfolded.

Somehow I doubted it.

More sirens came out of the water and their mouths began to move, but no sound came out. I knew, without being able to hear it, that they were singing. A strange urge came over me to remove the earplugs and just get a taste of their enchanting voices, but I pushed the feeling aside, recalling all the tales about sirens sending people to their deaths. This was one supernatural experience I was glad not to experience.

The sirens turned, coming toward us. For a second it felt

like I was in some kind of weird musical or flash mob. They all moved with an unnerving synchronicity. Add in their mouths moving as if singing, and all we needed was a stage to really get things going.

Deva backed up rapidly since she didn't have her earplugs in. We gave each other panicked looks and retreated with Deva so the sirens wouldn't know their song didn't affect us. As they drew closer, I could hear their song, as if they were singing from a great distance. It was beautiful, but it just didn't make me feel compelled to do anything. It was sad and mournful, as though they'd lost something great, something that was of immeasurable importance to them.

As we rose back up the path, gaining some elevation, and the boat came to the shore below, I was able to see down into the boat more clearly. And I recognized the shirt. I'd purchased it for him for his birthday a few years ago. It was bright red and had a picture of a game controller on it and then in bright white letters it read *Keep Calm and Blame it on the Lag*. That was definitely Henry. I'd bought it off some obscure internet store that catered to gamers, so it wasn't like every guy out there had one.

I tugged on my ear, the signal we'd decided to use if we wanted to attack. Beth slapped Deva lightly on her cheek. She shook her head and pulled her earplugs out of her pocket, stuffing them in her ears as fast as she could. The rest of us pulled our hair back, revealing our ear plugs.

"Give my brother back or face the consequences," I said in my biggest, baddest voice, leveling my take-no-bull stare on the female siren that had approached us. Was she a queen? A mayor? I had no idea, but clearly she was the one in command.

"Your brother killed a siren," the siren queen said. "We are owed a blood debt."

My stomach bottomed out and I wanted to throw up. Henry had killed someone? He had killed a siren?

No.

That wasn't possible, was it?

There wasn't a violent bone in his body. When the vampire had spoken about a blood debt, I'd assumed my brother accidentally hurt a siren. Not killed one. It didn't seem possible. Although, I hadn't known about his gambling either, so maybe I just had a blind spot when it came to my brother.

I didn't want to believe it though, so I glanced at my friends, all of whom looked just as shocked as me. None of us had expected this. None of us thought Henry was a killer either. In all our planning, we'd only discussed being able to reason with the sirens if he hurt one of them. The ladies had said that the sirens were crueler than the vampires and the shifters, but even they might hesitate to sacrifice a human who had ties to the supernatural world.

But in the books I'd read stories about people who had killed sirens. None of them survived once the other sirens found out. And the other supernaturals seemed to accept that one life for another was a fair exchange. I didn't think my friends would be able to stop the sirens if Henry had killed someone. I wasn't even sure if Karma could.

Now we just had to find out if it was true.

20

EMMA

"Hold up." I held my hands in the air. "That's not possible."

"If he actually killed a siren, he has to die. This is an ancient pact made between immortals to keep the peace. There's no way out of it." Beth's words were like daggers to my heart, each one of them.

I took a deep breath. There was no way Henry intentionally hurt someone. I *knew* it, knew my brother, and I wouldn't doubt him just because some fish lady said so.

The people—sirens?—in the boat pulled Henry out and carried him onto the shore, over the rocks. Now that I looked at them, the rocks lined the beach in a straight, perfect line. Like they were intentionally placed. They set him on his feet and maneuvered him toward us, presenting him to the siren in charge.

The men who carried Henry took off the black bag that covered his head and backed away, bowing slightly to the women. "Male sirens are submissive," Deva whispered.

Clearly.

"You must state your side of the events," she said, looking down at my brother somehow, even though he was a little taller than her. Her expression said she thought of him like something gross she'd stepped in. "It is our way."

Henry was clearly terrified. He was shaking like a leaf in the wind and had blood dried to his face. What had they done to him? The thought of them hurting my brother made a sob catch in my throat. Somehow, through all of this, I hadn't wanted to think about what he was going through during our search. Maybe it was because my brain just couldn't handle it, but now it was all I could think about.

That, and what would happen next. These people might think that if he killed someone his life would be forfeit, but Karma or no, I wouldn't let him be hurt. No matter what I had to do to stop it from happening.

"Speak!" the siren shouted, her eyes filled with fury.

My brother's gaze met mine. I swallowed down the sob building in my throat and steeled my face. If he saw I wasn't worried, I hoped it would give him the strength to explain himself, which was something he wasn't normally good at.

"Deep breath," I whispered.

He took a deep breath and a little of the panic eased from his expression.

"It was an accident," he began slowly, but with an edge of fear in his voice. "The vampires and shifters were chasing me, and a siren jumped out at me. I reacted by punching him. In the dark, I didn't even know he wasn't one of the people trying to hurt me. He fell back and hit his head and I didn't know it. But he died. I didn't know until they came and got me at home."

Henry's eyes were wild, and he tried to take a step toward me only to have the cord that bound his hands yanked on by one of the male sirens. It pulled him toward the male siren, making him stumble and almost fall.

The longer I looked at him the angrier I got. I understood grief, I knew the anger and denial and rage that it came with, but that was no excuse to execute someone for an accident. He'd been in these clothes for days and judging from the dirt and blood caked on his skin and the way his hair stuck up at various angles they hadn't given him a chance to clean himself. He looked bewildered by everything and as though he was about to pass out. I wasn't sure whether it was from fear or lack of food and water, since I was fairly sure they hadn't exactly been keeping him in good conditions.

"You left him to die," one of the sirens in the crowd said.

"Silence," the siren queen called. "Now we've heard the truth from your own mouth."

The siren queen turned to me. "You see? There is nothing you can do."

"No!" I screamed. Surging forward, I pushed past the two males that had been blocking the path and threw myself in front of Henry. "I didn't make the pact. It was an accident. I won't let this happen!"

The females seemed to just add me to the list of problems to be solved via murder. They formed a circle around us all, tightening it as they pushed my friends toward Henry and me. The female sirens all pulled out sacrificial daggers from belts I hadn't even noticed before, probably because I was too busy trying to keep my eyes on their faces or something equally polite like that.

The blades were curved in a wicked way on one end. There must have been a handle bit in the middle because the other end was a flat, short blade. The short end reminded me of what people used for shucking clams and oysters, while the other end looked like something out of one of Henry's video games. It looked excessively nasty.

Once they had all drawn their blades they began to speak, all at once. Creepy as fuck. "He is our blood sacrifice. He must die. He is our blood sacrifice. He must die."

The head siren stepped forward. She indicated the dry waterfall high above us as she said, "His sacrifice might undo the curse that stopped the sacred waters. Without the sacred water, we have been unable to have children. My people are dying. Our species will go extinct if we do not do this." Her gaze returned to me and narrowed. "More sacrifices will appease the gods, I do think. A male and a female. What could be more fitting? After your blood coats the basin, the water will start flowing once more and we will be bountiful with babes."

"Has it fixed this before?" I asked, heart racing.

The siren queen frowned. "Not yet. But perhaps we haven't appeased the gods yet."

"If past sacrifices haven't worked, why would this one?"

A smirk curled her lips. "It's worth the risk."

Deva, Carol, and Beth surged forward, but the male sirens appeared out of nowhere and pulled them backward. Apparently, even though we had been surrounded by the female sirens, we weren't part of the same group. Henry and I were being kept apart from my friends since we were the sacrifices.

We'd worn our charms and they hadn't helped. Well, maybe they had. I wasn't sure since no one had outright attacked us. I pulled on the hex bag Carol had given me, tearing it away from the leather necklace, and hurled it at the main siren. I had never been amazing at sports, but it was a pretty good throw if I said so myself. When she waved her arm and it fell to the ground unbroken I was more than a little disappointed.

I was also terrified.

What was I supposed to do now?

21

I only had one more trick up my sleeve.

I was a mom.

Pulling out my best mom-voice I said, "Now enough is enough. Put those daggers down right this instant!" The sirens actually hesitated, looking from me to their leader with uncertainty. I stacked my hands on my hips before I added, "You are jumping to a lot of conclusions here. Is this the best choice to make? Is it? How do you know that the sacrifices will please the gods? What if they just anger them even more?"

The lead siren rolled her eyes. "Stop that." She took a menacing step toward Henry.

"No, hang on." I held up my hands and shifted from foot to foot, moving slightly in front of Henry once more as I tried to think fast. "I'm Karma."

The siren queen's eyes widened a fraction before they narrowed on me in suspicion. "I thought that was a myth."

"Yeah, I get that a lot. But maybe there's something I can do about this curse." I winced internally for a moment, sure that calling the missing waterfall cursed would just piss them off even more, but they didn't react.

After a long pause where she just blinked at me with that creepy third eyelid, the siren queen said, "Karma is among the gods we worship. If you are indeed Karma embodied, we would allow you the opportunity to earn your brother's life."

I snorted before I could stop myself. "Well, I am. Give me a few minutes. Let me see what I can see about this water, okay? Can you do that for me?"

The siren queen exchanged a glance with one of the other females. "We can."

I wished they'd put their scary-looking blades away, but at least they dropped them to their sides. Glancing at Henry, I saw that he was watching me closely. He probably thought I was lying and had some kind of trick up my sleeve. Unfortunately for him, I wasn't lying, but I also wasn't sure that I could help the sirens with their problem. Luckily, my powers had served me well so far, so I could only hope they'd continue to do so.

I inched toward the dry waterfall. The circle of female sirens opened, and they let me have a path closer to the rocks lined up so neatly leading up to the empty falls. The way they formed a path forced me to walk a certain way, and I wasn't sure if it was because they only allowed people to approach the falls from a specific direction or if they were trying to intimidate me with how many of them there were. It was definitely more than had been there when I started talking to the siren queen.

The sand under my feet became hard packed and it was clear where the water used to be, but I wasn't entirely sure what to do. This wasn't like glaring at a jerk and watching them get punished. This was something deeper.

Karma, help me, I told myself, although I wasn't sure if it was the old lady or me who had a chance at fixing whatever was wrong here.

My gaze moved from the dry waterfall to the dry lake below, and then up higher to the cliffs that surrounded this area. Was it that there was less water in the mountains? Is that what stopped the waterfall? If I only saw the world without magic, the way I had most of my life, I'd assume that was the reason. But could this place really be cursed? Could it be something supernatural stopping the water?

I wasn't sure. And I wasn't sure how that would help the sirens get pregnant, but that wasn't really my concern. All I had to do is try to get the water flowing. Somehow.

Not knowing what else to do, I closed my eyes and touched the rocks that sat at the base of the waterfall. I wasn't sure exactly what I was doing, but I tried to focus on how it'd felt every time I used my magic. It seemed to be different each time. Something almost natural, like a reflex. So I concentrated on this place, to see if I could feel anything that was off.

To my surprise, I felt my magic spread out, tingling as it left my hand. I focused on the rocks and their history. Their heritage. What had they seen over all these years? What made the land stop providing for the sirens?

In my mind, I could see a thick black sludge laid across the rocks. I stiffened. It *was* a curse. Not just some natural thing that had made the water stop flowing. Now, I just needed to see if I could fix it.

I pushed past it, refusing to let the darkness of the curse overtake me. It was a strange feeling, like moving with my mind through quicksand. Or trying to work out a problem that sent goosebumps blossoming across my skin every time I drew closer to the solution. At times I felt entirely stuck, but I gritted my teeth and kept pushing forward, Henry's face in the back of my thoughts.

It didn't matter that I wasn't sure what I was doing. I had to figure out a solution, and quick.

When I broke through to the other side of the thing that had to be the curse, images assaulted me, one after another in rapid succession. I could see the connection the sirens had to the land and the waters here, and I could see how it had become twisted and deformed under their abuse. I could see how much they had taken and used without ever wondering if they should pay it back. They fished too much; they used the natural resources that had been provided to them like they were infinite, when in fact they were waning faster than any of us could imagine. It made my stomach clench and bile rise up the back of my throat.

Staggering backward, I faced the crowd of sirens, my brother, and my friends. "It was your greed and cruelty that stopped the waters."

They gasped, some looking offended.

Part of me wondered if it was smart to tell them the truth, but I couldn't seem to stop the words. "You *must* stop prioritizing money and other riches over your ancestral waters." To my shock, power filled my voice, weighing on the crowded sirens. They knelt as I spoke, almost like the power in my voice was too much for them to resist. The offense on some of their faces faded to wonder. "If you give a blood oath to restore the waters, to stop overfishing and polluting the waters, and to give back to the waters, I will let the sacred water flow loose again."

The siren queen stepped toward me, though her head was ever so slightly bowed. Her opinion of me had certainly changed in the last couple of minutes. "We will do whatever is needed."

The light of the moon glinted off the metal they had been brandishing at us not more than a few minutes ago, and I knew what needed to be done, even though I didn't know why. "Use those daggers," I commanded. "Give *your* blood to the stones. The sacrifice that needs to be made is from you, all of you, no one else." Every siren stood and without speaking formed a series of lines. Each one sliced their palm and pressed their hands to the sacred stones around the empty pool area as they approached, giving their blood as an oath.

I closed my eyes. I could actually feel the way the land responded to their blood. It rippled out into the forest and up the mountains to the source of their water. There was a moment, just a few short seconds, that I wasn't sure if it would work, where the mountain seemed reluctant to release the sacred waters that it had been guarding for so long. After a very long minute with nothing happening, I could sense the sirens behind me wondering if they'd been tricked. They were starting to think this had all been a ploy to buy myself time and were getting upset.

"You can do it," Deva called, her voice ringing out as clear as a bell in the stillness.

"We believe in you," Beth added, her voice filled with hope.

"I'm trying to help!" That was Carol. Almost at the same time as her words reached my ears, I felt her magic flow over me, giving me strength as I tried to pull the waters down from the mountain that was so far away. A second later, I felt the chill of the cool mountain air rush over my skin making me break out in goosebumps.

And then I felt the first water droplet against my skin. I lifted my face upward to search the top of the waterfall for any signs of the water the sirens so desperately needed.

Then another droplet fell, and another, and another. I squinted in the darkness but could see well enough by the light of the moon to watch the first few drops of water fall off the edge of the cliff face. Some of the sirens must have seen it too, because whispers started up behind me. When I saw that the drops were increasing in size and frequency, I knew I had to move. "Move," I called. "Hurry!"

I ran to the side, grabbing Henry's arm and yanking him with me as I moved.

Enough of the sirens must have realized that we had been successful because no one tried to prevent us from leaving the stones or the circle of sirens.

The siren queen led the way and all of the crowd rushed forward, standing at the base of the waterfall. I knew I shouldn't have been surprised by the sudden flow of water, but when it came roaring over the edge I couldn't help but gasp. It fell on the sirens below like they were standing under the oncoming tide. They began to dance and sing, frolicking in their ancestral waters as the rocky area filled with water for a moment before it overflowed into the ocean.

Fortunately, when I'd scurried out of the way, dragging Henry with me, my friends had taken the hint and moved to the side as well, which was why we all stood there together, watching this incredible moment.

A hand found my empty one, the one that wasn't holding on to Henry for dear life, and I looked over to see Beth watching with tears shimmering in her eyes. "I always wondered why they were so angry," Beth said. "But not being able to have children, that would anger anyone. I can't imagine the heartbreak they must have been going through."

I gave Beth's hand a squeeze and let go. It felt like there

was more there than I was comfortable asking about in front of strangers. Because I didn't know how to respond, I lifted Henry's hands and untied them before I threw my arms around him. "Henry, you are so done with gambling."

Before I could stop myself, I glanced over my shoulder and saw the siren queen watching us. I had honored my end of the bargain. Would she?

22

DANIEL

I stared at the flowing water in shock for several seconds before walking closer to the path that led to the beach. This waterfall had been dry for as long as I could remember. Now it flowed with life, the frothy churn of water covering it until it made it out to the ocean.

Moving closer to the edge, I looked down the path to see the base of the waterfall where the sirens, some in human form, some in their fins, danced and cheered as the water continued to splash over them and fill the little pooling area that had existed there since before I was born. Or at least it had until the waters dried up.

Before I could get too distracted by the mystery of the newly flowing waterfall, I glanced around. I had come here to save Henry after all, and with water flowing, did that mean I was too late?

The thought made the bear within me angry, and a low growl exploded from my lips. I'd spent nearly every minute since learning Henry was with the sirens talking to the siren liaisons and trying to arrange a meeting before the ceremony. I'd also gone back to talk to the vampires and the wolf shifters to try to find any connection between the sirens and Henry that I could. All I found was that Henry had really pissed them all off, but no one knew when he could've come in contact with a siren. Tonight, when I realized I was running out of time, I'd finally hung up on the jerk siren liaison and drove here as fast as I could.

I'd known this wasn't the first time the sirens had one of these ceremonies, even though I didn't have any proof. But this was the first time the waters were flowing in longer than I could remember. So had killing Henry been the thing to finally fix what was wrong here when other blood sacrifices hadn't worked? I didn't know, but magic and curses had always confused me.

My gut churned as the thought crossed my mind. I inched closer to the edge of the cliff, not seeing Henry's dark head of hair. I frowned, then looked straight under me. Then, thanks to the full moon, I saw Emma standing with her friends and Henry. Their hair was all much darker than the sirens. Even Beth's blonde hair looked dark in comparison.

"What in the hell," I whispered and rushed over to the path down to the beach.

Emma and company met me about halfway up. "Well, that's that," Emma said, a cheeky grin tugging at her lips. Her cheeks were flushed and her eyes glittered in the moonlight. She looked enchanting, and I couldn't help but wonder if it had something to do with getting Henry back. Was this what happiness looked like on her? If so, she wore it well. I might even go so far as to say better than most people.

"What are you?" I blurted, amazement taking my verbal filter away. I cleared my throat and tried again, keeping myself more composed the second time. "What did you do?" This erased any doubt in my mind that Emma had become something supernatural, because there was no way her friends had enough magic to do something like this. But what she was, I wasn't exactly sure. But I'd figure it out. That was kind of my thing, after all.

"Emma fixed it all," Deva said as she walked past me with that all-knowing smile she occasionally got on her face. She patted me on the shoulder. "Don't worry. It's all going to work itself out." Sometimes I couldn't help but wonder if there wasn't a little seer mixed in with Deva's witchy heritage. She always seemed to see more and know more than most people. It could be quite unnerving, or at least it would have been if I wasn't used to it already.

"Your gambling problem?" I asked, looking over at Henry as he went to walk past me without saying anything.

He shrugged as though he hadn't almost just died at the hands of sirens. Or that he hadn't almost cost his sister and her friends their lives as well. I wasn't sure how close it had come, but judging by the relief and sudden exhaustion on the women's faces, it was closer than I would have liked.

"But you're all okay?"

Emma gave a tired smile. "Yeah, we are. Thanks for coming, though."

I couldn't help but shake my head. "Usually I'm not just a few minutes behind the real problem-solvers."

She laughed. "I wouldn't call us that."

"No, but you do make a pretty great team if you can get the wolf cubs in order, face vampires, and save someone from a blood debt to the sirens."

Emma looked so damn proud as she glanced at her friends. "I guess you're right."

It was strange how amazed she seemed. Didn't she know,

powers or not, she had always been the kind of person who could work miracles? Like bringing an old bear out of his cave to help with a mystery, not that I'd done much.

"So how did you get the sirens to let Henry go? How did you get the waters to flow?"

She just smiled. "It's late. And it's been a long week."

Emma walked past me without answering my question about who or what she was and what she'd done. I wanted to be offended that she hadn't paid more attention to me and had ignored my questions, but I also knew how it went after a successful operation. It wasn't like Mystic Hollow was riddled with crime, but when I was a police officer I'd faced problems like this too. When the operations were over, most of the men were too busy riding an adrenaline high to write up accurate reports, so we had to institute an unofficial cool down period.

I'd let Emma cool off and enjoy the fact that Henry was safe, but soon enough I knew I would have to get to the bottom of this. Anyone who could make these waters flow was incredibly powerful. I wasn't sure if that was good or bad for the town.

As they headed toward their car, I had the feeling Henry was going to get the scolding of his lifetime in between hugs and slaps. He deserved it all. The guy was crazy smart, but that didn't mean he couldn't also be incredibly stupid. I hoped that he'd learned his lesson and wasn't going to gamble with the vamps and shifters any more. But if he actually had a problem, an addiction, then we were all in for a tougher fight. I wouldn't envy Emma or Henry's girlfriend, Alice, the job of keeping him on the straight and narrow.

The women were jovial as they climbed into the car, three of them stuffing themselves in the back seat with

Henry in the front passenger next to Beth, who looked happier than I'd seen her in a long time. I was happy myself, relieved that Henry was alive and not being turned into fish food.

With the weight of Henry's life off my shoulders, I walked down the rocky, sandy path toward the sirens. As I expected, one of the males branched off and stopped me before I got close. "You cannot interfere."

I held up my hands. "Not trying to interfere. I'm just wondering what happened here?" I asked.

I'd seen this siren before. He sold trinkets on the town pier, most of which were made from what he had scavenged from the ocean floor, or at least that was my guess. In any case, the two of us had interacted before, which I thought might have been the only reason he deigned to answer my question.

"A goddess restored our ancient waters," he replied. "It was meant to be." His gaze shifted to something over my shoulder and I was fairly sure that if I looked it would be the direction the women had disappeared in. And I had the sneaking suspicion that the goddess he was referring to was Emma. I mean, she was beautiful, but a goddess?

The hairs on the back of my neck stood on end. I couldn't resist any longer, so I turned and followed the direction of the siren's gaze, looking up the path to see the car backing out before pulling away. She was obviously immensely powerful. Did she know how dangerous that could be?

Power like that wasn't just something that was used occasionally. It could call to people who wanted it, seduce them into trying to take it. There would be others that would feel her strength eventually and come looking for her, hoping to take her power, whatever it was, for themselves. Would she be able to stop them? Or would she gladly turn it over to them, more than ready to return to the human she had been in high school?

I had no idea. But I'd do whatever I could to help protect her. I just hoped it would be enough.

23

EMMA

"Can you drop me at Alice's house?" Henry asked.

I sighed and glared at him but nodded. "Sure, yeah." Apparently his older sister saving his butt still didn't make me cool enough for him to want to hang out with me. Not that Henry had ever cared about how cool I was, but still, I guess part of me had thought we would spend some time together once he was safe.

I should have known that Alice would be his first port of call. Sisters ranked somewhere way below girlfriends, even at our age.

Beth stopped the car in front of Alice's house, or rather her parents' house, since she still lived with them.

Henry turned and met each of our eyes one by one. "Thank you," he whispered. "Thank you so much."

"Hey," Deva said using her best mom voice. "Keep yourself out of trouble." She patted Henry on the shoulder and he flinched like she'd stabbed him. I guessed it would take some time to get over whatever the sirens did to him.

"Enough gambling!" Carol said as she swatted him on the shoulder.

"Don't be out too late," I added, not wanting to say that my nerves were shot after today and that if he didn't come home I might assume that the siren queen, who had introduced herself to me as Ariquia before we left, had decided to take that blood payment after all. I didn't honestly think she would change her mind, but I also knew how my mind worked and how it would jump to the worst possible conclusion after something like this.

Henry merely nodded at me before getting out and bounding up the front steps of Alice's house. Beth waited to see him knock on the door. When Alice opened it, her face lit up and she threw her arms around Henry's neck. Suddenly I felt like a jerk for wanting him to spend time with me and not her. They obviously adored each other. We pulled away once the door shut behind them and made the short trip back to my place.

As soon as we walked into the house, I went for the kitchen and grabbed a bottle of wine from the fridge. "If ever we've deserved some celebratory wine, it's now." I rummaged through the drawer next to the fridge for the bottle opener.

Deva appeared next to me and ran her finger up one side and down the other of the bottle. "Now it won't run out for the next couple of hours."

Once I had the bottle open I carried it and the glasses over to the table rather awkwardly before pouring four glasses and handing them out to my friends. We sat around the kitchen table and sighed, relaxing for the first time all week.

"To Emma," Deva said. "We are so happy to have you as a part of our coven."

"And if you officially join our business, you can be paid

and help us. And we can help you figure out your magic. Honing it, making it stronger," Beth added.

I nodded eagerly. "I'm in! Totally in." It sounded amazing. I couldn't help but be gleeful. I had a real future, a real reason to look forward to waking up tomorrow for the first time in *so* many years.

"Before we have too much wine, I have a present for you," Deva said.

My brows furrowed. A present? After I'd been a crappy friend for all these years?

"Stop looking like that. I knew you'd get your brother back tonight. In fact, I was so confident that I made up this necklace for you."

"Necklace?" I asked, just getting more confused.

"It's a protection charm, but it's not so much for you as it is for Henry." Deva pulled one of her rings off and flicked the stone.

The whole thing opened up, kind of like a locket. Inside there was a short needle and what I could only assume was a drop of blood. There was nothing else in the world that was quite the same color as blood. Deva pulled a necklace from her purse and set it on the table, dripping the contents of the ring onto the pendant. It sizzled and the blood seemed to be absorbed into the metal until there wasn't a trace of it left.

"There," she said a moment later. "Now, if Henry gets hurt you will know. This pendant will warm against your skin, letting you know he's in trouble. That way we can react as quickly as possible."

"Was that his blood?" I asked, dumbfounded.

Deva nodded. "I just gave him a pat on the shoulder with this, and it collected what I needed to activate the pendant." She waved the ring in the air before slipping it back on her finger. There was no way I would have guessed that it held a needle inside, or that it would shoot out and collect someone's blood.

Relief coursed through me. "Thank you. This is--I--"

Before I could continue to stumble over my words, the doorbell rang. I took another long gulp of wine and secretly wondered if maybe it was Daniel at the door. I hoped so. "Be right back."

When I opened the front door, a piece of paper fluttered to the ground. I left it there and stepped onto the front porch, but in the dark, with the roof shielding us from the light of the moon, I couldn't see anyone around. I gave the neighborhood a long, narrow-eyed stare, as though I was getting ready to scold it, before picking up the paper and going back inside. Whoever dropped it off had hightailed it out of there faster than I would have thought possible. I was exhausted though, so maybe I was moving slower than I thought.

My mood was still light and happy. I opened the paper and gasped. In an instant, my happy, hopeful future crashed around me like a ton of bricks.

I know what you did. You're going to pay.

"What is it?" Carol asked as I stumbled back into the kitchen, barely making sure the door was latched and locked behind me.

"It's about my ex husband," I whispered.

Beth took the note and almost immediately dropped it on the table. "Whoever wrote it is *full* of power. I mean overflowing."

Deva held her hand over it. "I feel it too. What did you do?"

They all looked at me with wide, worried eyes. Beth gave me a pointed look that said it was time to share the full story of what happened when I became karma with my other friends. I'd let it slip when it was just Beth and I, but ever since then I'd tried to keep quiet about it. I still felt guilty about what I'd done, even if they deserved it, and I didn't know what kind of ramifications doing something like that had in the supernatural world. Hell, I hadn't even known the supernatural world existed when it had happened.

I sighed and slumped down at the table, pulling my wine to me and taking a long, fortifying drink. I had to tell them the truth if I hoped to get their help getting myself out of this. "Once upon a time, a woman accidentally turned her ex husband and his new girlfriend into toads. Turns out she wasn't living in the fairy tale she thought, and now the evil witch is after her."

Their eyes widened, and I took a long sip of my wine.

I saved Henry. But now, somehow, I needed to save myself.

Did you enjoy this book? If so, preorder book two, **Karma's Shift.**

ALSO BY HELEN SCOTT

Don't forget to check out Helen's other series.

Immortal Hunters MC (Cowritten with Lacey Carter Andersen)

Van Helsing Rising

Van Helsing Damned - Coming Soon

Magical Midlife in Mystic Hollow (Cowritten with Lacey Carter Andersen and LA Boruff)

Karma's Spell

Karma's Shift - Coming Soon

The Wild Hunt

Daughter of the Hunt

Challenger of the Hunt

Champion of the Hunt – Coming Soon

Prisoners of Nightstone (Cowritten with May Dawson)

Potions and Punishments

Incantations and Inmates - Coming Soon

Twisted Fae

(Cowritten with Lucinda Dark)

Court of Crimson

Court of Frost

Court of Midnight

The Hollow

(Cowritten with Ellabee Andrews)

Survival

Seduction

Surrender

Salsang Chronicles

(cowritten with Serena Akeroyd)

Stained Egos

Stained Hearts

Stained Minds

Stained Bonds

Stained Souls

Salsang Chronicles Box Set

Cerberus

Daughter of Persephone

Daughter of Hades

Queen of the Underworld

Cerberus Series Box Set

Hera's Gift (A Cerberus Series Novella)

Four Worlds

Wounding Atlantis

Finding Hyperborea

Escaping El Dorado

Embracing Agartha – Coming Soon

Wardens of Midnight

Woman of Midnight (A Wardens of Midnight Novella)

Sanctuary at Midnight

The Siren Legacy

The Oracle (A Siren Legacy Novella)

The Siren's Son

The Siren's Eyes

The Siren's Code

The Siren's Heart

The Banshee (A Siren Legacy Novella)

The Siren's Bride

Fury's Valentine (A Siren Legacy Novella)

Standalones, Shared Worlds, and Box Sets

The Sex Tape

Spin My Gold (Cowritten with Lacey Carter Andersen)

Buttercup

Neve

ALSO BY LACEY CARTER

A Supernatural Midlife

The Ghost Hunter

The Shifter Hunter

The Fairy Hunter

A Supernatural Midlife- The Complete Collection

Magical Midlife in Mystic Hollow

Karma's Spell

Karma's Shift

Karma's Spirit

Karma's Stake

Shifting Into Midlife

Pack Bunco Night

Alpha Males and Other Shift

An Immortal Midlife

Fatal Forty

Fighting Forty

Finishing Forty

ALSO BY L.A. BORUFF

A Ghoulish Midlife (Paranormal Women's Fiction co-write with Lia Davis) https://laboruff.com/books/witching-after-forty/

The Unseen War (Paranormal Reverse Harem): https://laboruff.com/books/unseen/

Valentine Pride (Complete Paranormal Reverse Harem co-write with Laura Greenwood): https://laboruff.com/books/valentine/

Coven's End (Complete Paranormal Reverse Harem co-write with Lia Davis): https://laboruff.com/books/ce/

Academy's Rise (Paranormal Reverse Harem co-write with Lia Davis): https://laboruff.com/books/ar/

Lucifer's War (Paranormal Romance co-write with Lia Davis):
https://laboruff.com/books/lucifers-war/

Tales of Clan Robbins (Paranormal Western Romance co-write with Laura Greenwood):
https://laboruff.com/books/the-tales-of-clan-robbins/

The Firehouse Feline (Paranormal Comedic Reverse harem co-write with Laura Greenwood and Lacey Carter Andersen): https://laboruff.com/books/the-firehouse-feline/

Magic & Metaphysics Academy (Paranormal Academy Reverse Harem co-write with Laura Greenwood):
https://laboruff.com/books/m-m

Southern Soil (Sweet Contemporary Reverse Harem): https://laboruff.com/books/southernsoil/

ABOUT THE AUTHOR

Helen Scott lives in the Chicago area with her wonderful husband and furry, four-legged kids. She spends way too much time with her nose in a book and isn't sorry about it. When not reading or writing, Helen can be found absorbed in one video game or another or crafting her heart out.

Thank you for reading!
You can also come and hang out in my reader group, Helen's Hellraisers, where you can find out all about what I'm working on, sneak peeks, and even exclusive giveaways!
Come and join the fun here!
Don't want to join the group but want to know what's going on?
Follow me on social media:
Website: http://www.helenscottauthor.com
Facebook: http://www.facebook.com/helenscottauthor/
Twitter: http://twitter.com/HelenM459
Instagram: http://www.instagram.com/helenscottauthor/
Don't forget to sign up for my newsletter for new release alerts, giveaways, and other fun stuff!

ABOUT THE AUTHOR

L.A. (Lainie) Boruff lives in East Tennessee with her husband, three children, and an ever growing number of cats. She loves reading, watching TV, and procrastinating by browsing Facebook. L.A.'s passions include vampires, food, and listening to heavy metal music. She once won a Harry Potter trivia contest based on the books and lost one based on the movies. She has two bands on her bucket list that she still hasn't seen: AC/DC and Alice Cooper. Feel free to send tickets.

ABOUT THE AUTHOR

Lacey Carter writes paranormal women's fiction and cozy mysteries with humor, adventure, and a little romance. Her stories are sure to make you smile, laugh, and maybe even cry. But don't worry, she's always sure to give her readers a happy ending for her brave heroes and heroines.

As a USA Today bestselling author, Lacey is always working on another story. She thrives off of the adventure both in her books and outside of them, while raising her three beautiful children, with her amazing husband. She also writes steamy romances under the name Lacey Carter Andersen.

So if you're looking for fun and adventure, dive into one of her worlds today!

Made in the USA
Columbia, SC
10 July 2022